PASSION PLAY

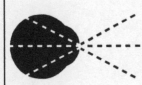

This Large Print Book carries the
Seal of Approval of N.A.V.H.

PASSION PLAY

REGINA HART

THORNDIKE PRESS
A part of Gale, Cengage Learning

GALE
CENGAGE Learning·

Farmington Hills, Mich • San Francisco • New York • Waterville, Maine
Meriden, Conn • Mason, Ohio • Chicago

GALE
CENGAGE Learning·

LIBRARY OF CONGRESS CATALOGING-IN-PUBLICATION DATA

Names: Hart, Regina, author.
Title: Passion play / Regina Hart.
Description: Waterville, Maine : Thorndike Press Large Print, 2016. | © 2016 | Series: The Anderson family ; 2 | Series: Thorndike Press large print African-American.
Identifiers: LCCN 2015044724| ISBN 9781410485786 (hardback) | ISBN 1410485781 (hardcover)
Subjects: LCSH: African Americans—Fiction. | Large type books. | BISAC: FICTION / Romance / Contemporary. | GSAFD: Love stories.
Classification: LCC PS3608.A7867 P378 2016 | DDC 813/.6—dc23
LC record available at http://lccn.loc.gov/2015044724

Published in 2016 by arrangement with Harlequin Books S.A.

Printed in Mexico
1 2 3 4 5 6 7 20 19 18 17 16

To my dream team:
My sister, Bernadette,
for giving me the dream
My husband, Michael,
for supporting the dream
My brother Richard
for believing in the dream
My brother Gideon
for encouraging the dream
And to Mom and Dad
always with love.

CHAPTER 1

"Ben is on my panel." Rose Beharie dropped that bombshell on her two younger sisters during their weekly Wednesday family dinner. What kind of perverse wench was Fate that she'd pair her with her snake of an ex-fiancé on her law school reunion's legislative presentation panel?

"Are you kidding me?" Her youngest sister, Iris, recovered from the surprise first. Seated beside Rose, Iris stared at her, wide-eyed.

Rose had met Benjamin Shippley during their first year of law school at the University of Michigan. She'd thought he was The One. Instead, he was one of the biggest mistakes she'd ever made. She must have been insane to register for her ten-year law school reunion without first learning whether Benjamin would be attending. Temporary insanity — or more likely hubris.

She'd read in their alumni e-newsletter

that Benjamin and his bride of almost one year lived in Los Angeles. He was an entertainment lawyer. *Whatever.* Rose was now a partner at one of the most prestigious firms in Ohio. Since they practiced such different types of law, Rose would never have pictured them participating on the same reunion panel. Had someone deliberately put them together? If so, who? Why? And did that person have exceptional health insurance?

"What are you going to do?" Her middle sister, Lily, paused with her glass of iced cucumber water halfway to her mouth. She was seated across the table from Rose.

After their parents had died, Lily had suggested the three of them continue the weekly Beharie family meals. Rose and Iris returned to their family home — now Lily's home — every Wednesday for dinner, conversation and sibling support.

That's what Rose needed now. "I have to find a date for the reunion."

"Why?" Lily finished her tilapia.

"I've already registered and agreed to serve on the panel." Rose moved her green beans to another side of her plate. A deep breath carried to her the savory aroma of seasoned tilapia. "I can't back out now. Ben will think I'm not over him."

"But you *are* over him. You're *so* over

8

him." Iris, her youngest sister, glowered as she stuffed a green bean into her mouth.

"I know." Rose glared at her half-full plate. Instead of the wonderful meal Lily had cooked, all Rose tasted was the anger, hurt and bitterness of her words. "I want Ben to know it, too. That's why I need a date."

"Someone to make Ben eat his heart out." Iris grinned with evil intent.

Rose stared at the original artwork on the wall behind Lily. It was of a scarlet vase of wildflowers. "Someone handsome, successful, charming."

"And rich." Iris sipped her cucumber water.

"I don't understand." Lily slid aside her empty dinner plate. "You're going to bring some stranger to your reunion and pass him off as your fake boyfriend so Ben will know you're over him? What is this, some sort of low-budget TV movie of the week?"

"No, it's revenge." Iris drained her glass of water.

"Ben was cheating on me even before he proposed." Rose shoved aside her half-full plate and leaned into the table. "Do you have any idea how that made me feel?"

"No, I don't. But I know how it made *me* feel." Lily's voice was quiet. "And I know how it makes me feel to see you still so hurt and upset. Rose, you don't have to miss the reunion. You don't have to bring a fake boyfriend to it, either. There's a third option."

"What?" Rose regarded her sister closely.

"You could go by yourself." Lily folded her hands on the table.

Rose's eyes widened. "I can't go to the reunion by myself."

"Come on, Lil." Iris added her voice to Rose's. "It's been sixteen months. Ben can't know that Rosie hasn't even had a date in more than a year."

"Thanks, Iris." Rose's response cracked with sarcasm. Having her youngest sister put her fears into words made Rose feel worse. But Iris was right. She didn't want Benjamin to know she hadn't had anyone else in her life since she'd kicked him out.

A sudden restlessness overcame Rose. She stood and gathered Lily's and Iris's dishes and silverware, in addition to her own. She sensed her sisters behind her as she carried the load into the kitchen. Rose's eyes moved over the familiar pale gold walls, blond wood furnishings and stainless steel appliances. Lily had done little to redecorate their family home. Was it because, like her, Lily found comfort in the surroundings?

"Rosie, you're a successful, intelligent and

10

beautiful woman." The impatience in Lily's voice took away from the compliment. "You don't need a boyfriend — fake or otherwise — to be complete."

"You're not getting it, Lil." Iris returned the place mats to the marble kitchen counter.

"I appreciate the sentiment." Rose stacked the plates and silverware into the dishwasher. "But if I show up to the reunion alone, people will talk. Some will even snicker." Her skin grew cold just imagining the negative reactions: stares, whispers, condescension.

Lily carried her step stool to the counter. She mounted the stool, then dug out a plastic storage bowl from the honey-wood cabinet above the stainless steel stove. "You're acting as though none of your former classmates would be supportive of you. What about those friends you get together with every month?"

"They would be supportive." To a point.

The Constant Classmates — they hadn't changed much over the years — were three of Rose's closest friends from her law school class. They were smart, successful, ambitious, condescending, narcissistic and competitive.

"I don't know why you're still friends with

11

them." Iris returned the pitcher of cucumber water to the side-by-side refrigerator. "You don't really like them."

"You guys have only met them once." Rose continued to carefully load the dishwasher. Lily was very particular about the arrangement of the dishes. "I know they come across as a little full of themselves."

"A little?" Iris snorted.

Rose gave her youngest sister a look. "We were study partners in law school. I wouldn't have made it without them. And they were very supportive when I found out about Ben."

Lily blew a dismissive breath. "You shouldn't allow other people to make you feel bad if you want to go to the reunion on your own."

"But I *don't* want to go alone." Rose faced Lily. "I want to go with a date."

"Then I hope you find someone before the reunion." Lily carried the dirty pans to the sink and filled them with soapy hot water. "Just let it happen, though. Don't plan to bring a phony boyfriend."

Rose straightened from the dishwasher, shutting the appliance's door. "I don't have time to depend on chance. The reunion is the weekend of September 18. That's only three months away."

"Those three months will just fly by." Iris carried the baking pan to the sink and began cleaning it.

"Thanks, Iris." Rose cut her baby sister another look.

"What are you going to do?" Lily propped her hips against the counter. Her blue terrycloth shorts hung to midthigh. A purple tulip featured prominently on her white cotton T-shirt. "Put an ad in a newspaper?"

"I was hoping you or Iris knew someone suitable." Rose rested her hips against the counter, facing her sisters. "I don't know any men outside of work, and I don't want to invite someone from the firm."

"I'm dating the only handsome, successful, charming, wealthy guy I know." Iris's smile was satisfied.

Iris's boyfriend, Tyler Anderson, was vice president of product development for Anderson Adventures, a family-owned computer gaming company. They'd met three months ago when Tyler hired Iris's solo marketing and public relations consulting firm, The Beharie Agency, to help launch his company's soon-to-be-released game, Osiris' Journey.

"This is a bad idea." Lily shook her head. "You're giving Ben too much power. It doesn't matter what he thinks. You know

13

that you don't need a man to validate you."

"I do know that." Rose sighed again. "But I really need you to support me in this plan. I'm sure it's not an accident that Ben and I are on the same presentation panel. Someone deliberately put us together. I don't want to show up alone."

Iris crossed to Rose and rested a hand on her shoulder. "If Rosie shows up alone, it will seem as though she hasn't gotten over Ben."

With or without Lily's approval, Rose was moving forward with her plan. But she really wanted both of her sisters' support. The three of them had always been close, even more so since their parents had died. Iris understood. Why couldn't Lily? Tension bunched in Rose's shoulders as she waited for her younger sister's response.

Finally, Lily turned. "If you're going to do this, be sure the man you get to play your fake boyfriend is handsome enough to make Ben jealous."

Rose smiled her relief. "That's the plan."

"I need a lawyer." Donovan Carroll sat on the gray cushioned guest chair in Xavier Anderson's office at Anderson Adventures. He balanced one of his company's oversize coffee mugs on his right thigh. It was a match to the mugs Xavier and Tyler were using.

The tension that dropped into the room after his announcement was tangible. From behind his desk, Xavier's gaze sprang from his mug to lock onto Donovan. In the matching seat beside him, Tyler, Xavier's cousin, nearly choked on his coffee.

"Why do you need a lawyer?"

"What's going on?"

Xavier and Tyler spoke at the same time. The concern in their voices was a reminder that, although he wasn't related to the Andersons by blood or marriage, they'd accepted him as family since he'd first met the cousins in college.

It was just after 7:00 a.m. on the third Thursday in June. Anderson Adventures was quiet. Very few employees arrived this early. Xavier, the company's vice president of finance, hadn't been the same since his recent breakup with his girlfriend. The reason his five-month relationship ended probably disturbed Xavier more than the actual breakup. For that reason, he and Tyler had agreed to start their mornings with Xavier to show their support.

Donovan drew a deep breath, collecting his thoughts. The scent of strong coffee clung to the air. "A pawnshop is trying to

15

move into one of the vacant storefronts in the same neighborhood where our shelters are located."

In his life away from Anderson Adventures, Donovan, the company's vice president of sales, served as president of the board of directors of Hope Homeless Shelter in downtown Columbus, Ohio.

Once his friends realized Donovan wasn't in trouble, the tension dissipated.

"I'd read in the newspaper that Public Pawn had plans to expand its locations." Xavier rolled up the sleeves of his dark blue jersey.

"I hadn't realized the company had chosen its first expansion location." Tyler drank more of his coffee.

"The board has been monitoring the pawnshop's progress. The owner made the announcement at the end of the day, after news deadlines." Donovan sighed. "We want a lawyer's help writing and filing a statement with the Columbus City Council against the pawnshop moving into our neighborhood."

"How much time do you have?" Tyler appeared calm in his dark brown polo shirt and tan Dockers. Usually the workaholic vice president of product development was itching to get back to work after ten minutes. But since he'd started dating Iris Beharie, Tyler had become more relaxed — and also more productive.

"Our response is due next month, the third week of July. We have four weeks to find a lawyer who can research, write and file our statement, all pro bono." *Piece of cake.* Donovan's natural wit failed to find the humor in this situation.

Xavier leaned back on his black leather executive chair. "Maybe our legal counsel has someone on staff who could help you."

Donovan had considered contacting their legal counsel but then dismissed the idea. "The board can't afford their rate, and I don't want to ask them for any favors. That would compromise Anderson Adventures' relationship with them in the future."

Xavier's dark eyebrows knitted. "What's the shelter's legal-aid budget?"

"It's somewhere between zero and a prayer." Donovan scrubbed his left hand over his face. "The shelter recently transferred its legal-aid funds into an operating account."

"Wow." Tyler arched his eyebrows. "It sounds like they were faced with tough budget choices — preserve a legal fund they may not need or pay immediate bills."

"Exactly." Donovan nodded. "Frankly, we

17

need a lawyer who would represent us pro bono."

Xavier exchanged a look with Tyler before meeting Donovan's eyes. "That could prove difficult."

"I know." Donovan drummed his fingers against the arms of his chair as he scanned the room.

Like Tyler's office, Xavier's space was meticulous. Black three-ring program binders were arranged on the shelf above the desk behind him. On his back wall, project folders were neatly arranged in a black metal file sorter on top of a three-foot-tall cabinet.

"Didn't you date a lawyer?" Tyler cocked his head as though searching his memory. "What was her name again?"

"Whitley Maxwell." She was attractive, intelligent and shallow.

"Whitley, that's right." Tyler snapped his fingers. "Maybe you could ask her to help."

"You've still got a lot to learn, Ty, if you think that would be a good idea." Xavier snorted.

"We didn't exactly part on good terms." Donovan glanced at Tyler. Had he brought up Whitley in an effort to amuse Xavier? His smile was faint, but it was the first sign of levity his friend had shown in more than a week.

Tyler shrugged. "She's a good lawyer and you know her."

"You're right." It wasn't that Whitley hadn't crossed his mind. But he was reluctant to return to any sort of relationship with her, considering the way their relationship had ended. "But she may be more trouble than she's worth."

"Maybe she's changed." Tyler's voice was pensive.

"Can people really change that much?" Xavier asked.

Donovan studied the other man. He sensed Xavier was thinking about his ex-girlfriend when he posed that question.

He turned back to Tyler. "I'll see if the other board members have luck finding a lawyer to help us pro bono. If not, I'll give Whitley a call."

He hoped the other members had a long list of recommendations for legal representation. He'd much rather not have to reconnect with his ex-girlfriend.

Rose was the last of the four former law school classmates to arrive at the Ethiopian restaurant after work Friday evening. She wasn't late. In fact, she was almost ten minutes early. What time had the others gotten off work?

"Sorry to keep you waiting." Rose offered the apology as she sat beside Maxine Ellerson in the booth.

"I just got here myself." Maxine was the least neurotic of the three other women. Her neat, close-cut natural complemented her pixie, coffee features.

Rose's companions had their drinks — a water, an iced tea and a lemonade. She waited as they gave their dinner requests to their waitress. The entire table ordered vegetable entrées, as usual. Rose was tempted to mix it up and order a meat dish. Instead she ordered the same thing she always did when they met once a month: the lentil salad, Azifa, and a glass of ice water with lemon.

While they waited for their dinners, Rose listened as the other lawyers brought each other up-to-date on personal and professional events. Maxine was a junior partner with a law firm not far from the restaurant in the Short North neighborhood. She'd been dating a chemist for the past several years. Tasha Smalls was unhappily married with two young children. She was legal counsel for a financial institution headquartered in downtown Columbus. Claudia

20

Brentwood-Washington had her own practice in the suburbs, and never missed an opportunity to boast about her well-trained husband and prodigy daughter.

Why do I do this to myself? Rose's gaze chased around the warm, vibrant colors of the restaurant's traditional decor. The air was fragrant with exotic spices, well-seasoned meats and savory stews. Their dinner conversation always reminded Rose of everything she should have had. She wasn't married. She wasn't even dating anyone. She was happy with her job at the law firm, but she wanted more. *Why am I here?*

Their conversation was briefly interrupted as the server brought their entrées, then Rose returned her attention to her former classmates.

She'd met them during their first year at law school while attending a Black Student Union meeting. Despite their different backgrounds and personalities, they'd stayed in touch over the past ten years, mainly through emails and these once-a-month dinners.

Tasha shook her head, sending her long, thin braids over her shoulder. "Rose, I felt so sorry for you when I heard that Ben was added to your legislative update panel for our reunion. How are you holding up?"

21

That didn't take long.

Rose lifted her eyes to hold Tasha's dark gaze. There was a time when she would have believed the innocent expression on the other woman's round, nutmeg face. But now she recognized the satisfied glint in Tasha's eyes. "Ben and I were over a long time ago."

"What are you going to do?" Claudia always looked as though she'd just walked out of a salon. How could she maintain a solo practice, care for her family and look perpetually perfect?

"Why do I have to do anything?" Rose shrugged one shoulder, feigning indifference. She swallowed a forkful of her salad. The savory dish tasted like ashes. Her ruined appetite was one more sin to count against Benjamin.

Claudia and Tasha exchanged incredulous looks.

Seated beside Rose, Maxine sipped her iced tea. "Ben probably got himself assigned to Rose's panel for the exposure, hoping she'd once again make him look good."

Rose lowered her gaze to her barely touched salad. Long ago she'd come to the same conclusion: Benjamin had used her success and popularity at their law school to meet people who could help him. She'd been so in love with the snake in disguise that she hadn't realized he'd only been interested in her body and her connections, not necessarily in that order.

"When did you finally notice he'd only been using you?" Tasha's question echoed her thoughts.

Maxine forked up her salad. "We're supposed to be getting caught up on each other's news. Why are we reliving the past?"

Rose glanced at Maxine, grateful for her intervention. However, Tasha wasn't done.

"Talking about Ben does qualify as catching up with Rose." Tasha pinned Rose with another watchful stare. "After all, finding out you'll be presenting with him during our reunion is your latest news, isn't it, Rose?"

"Actually, it's not." The words were out before Rose knew she was going to say them.

"What do you mean?" Claudia's warm brown eyes sparked with curiosity.

"You have other news?" Tasha was caught off guard. It was a rare occurrence for her.

"Don't keep us in suspense." Maxine nudged Rose's arm. "What is it?"

The moment of truth. Rose took a long drink of her ice water with lemon, then forced out the words. "I'm dating someone."

Maxine smiled into Rose's eyes. "Tell us about him. How did you meet?"

"What does he do?" Claudia leaned forward.

"Is he for real?" Tasha hid her sneer behind a tight smile.

Rose met the challenge in her friendly adversary's almond-shaped eyes. "What makes you think he's not?"

Tasha spread her hands. "Why are we only now hearing about him?"

"I didn't want to tell anyone until I knew whether he was serious." Not bad for an on-the-spot response. Rose gave herself a mental round of applause.

"That makes sense." Maxine set aside her nearly empty salad plate.

"I understand." Claudia sipped her iced tea. "You want to take your time."

"Exactly." Rose nodded as she finished off her salad.

The young server returned to clear away their empty plates and leave behind their individual bills.

"Why don't you tell us about him now?" Tasha's smile was a taunt. She checked her bill, then inserted her platinum credit card into the black leather bill holder.

"I'm still not ready." Rose added her card to her bill holder, as well. "But hopefully you'll have a chance to meet him during the reunion."

Their server returned to collect their bills. Rose searched her brain for a change of topic.

"Meeting your new boyfriend at the reunion should be interesting." Tasha's shoulders shook with her laughter.

Rose frowned. "Why?"

Tasha shrugged. "Because Ben will meet his replacement —"

"He's not Ben's replacement." Rose's tone was sharp. Was Tasha deliberately poking her temper?

"And you'll meet Ben's new wife." Tasha drank her diet soda. "Did you know she's pregnant?"

The temperature in the café seemed to drop by at least ten degrees. There was a buzzing in Rose's ears. "Ben's wife is pregnant?"

"You didn't know?" Tasha tilted her head. "She may be too far along to attend the reunion."

A shaft of hurt and anger so sharp sliced through Rose like scalding steel cleaving her in two. She clenched her teeth against the pain. Benjamin was living the life he'd promised her.

"Well, I wish them every happiness." The

lie was sour in her throat. She didn't want him to be happy. She wanted to hurt him back.

"Good for you, Rose." Maxine saluted her with her iced tea. "You've moved on and gotten over Ben."

That sounded like something Lily would say. The realization made Rose uncomfortable with her deception. Her gaze drifted away. Their server returned with their credit card receipts.

"It's getting late." Rose checked her silver wristwatch. "I'd better get going. It was great to see everyone."

Claudia stood. "At least show us a photo of this mystery man."

Rose chuckled as she stood, as well. "I don't carry his photo."

"You don't want to talk about him. You don't carry his photo." Tasha led them from the restaurant. "I have doubts that he really exists. I hope we meet him before the reunion."

Rose's shoulders tensed. *So do I.*

CHAPTER 2

"I need a boyfriend." Rose puffed the words as she and Iris continued their five-mile jog through the Park of Roses on Saturday morning.

It was the last day of spring, the day before the longest day of the year. Even this early on a Saturday morning, the park was busy with cyclists, walkers and other runners. Rose jogged beside Iris past the tennis courts. The row of maple trees on their left formed a canopy over them. They continued down the incline to the music of the birdsong around them.

"I thought you'd given up on men." Iris's strides were synchronized to Rose's, the result of years of jogging together.

Her youngest sister's lemon-yellow jersey and navy blue biker shorts were cheerful contrasts to Rose's steel-gray jersey and black shorts. They veered to the right at the bottom of the hill.

"A fake one for my reunion. Remember?" Rose frowned into the distance. Ben's fair features and wavy dark hair superimposed themselves over the park's picnic area. She briefly squeezed her eyes shut to dispel the objectionable image.

"Do you have any candidates?" Iris's voice became increasingly breathless as she expended more energy on the path.

"Not even one." Rose had searched her mind Friday night after dinner with her former classmates: work, church, neighbors, anyone.

"What about Leroi? You've worked with him for years."

"He's dating someone." Rose leaned forward and shortened her stride as she climbed the incline that led to the high school. Her words came out in puffs. "Besides, Leroi's successful. And intelligent. And good-looking. But he doesn't. Hold a candle. To Ben." And she needed someone whose looks would eclipse her ex-fiancé's.

"You're in luck." Iris took a breath. "I know someone. He'd be perfect. For your assignment."

"Who?" Rose crested the hill with Iris. Her pulse and breathing slowly returned to normal.

"Donovan Carroll. Also goes by 'Van.'

He's Ty's friend. Vice president of sales. For Anderson Adventures."

"How's he look?" Rose looked at Iris, reluctant to believe her sister had the answer to her problem.

"Six-three, six-four. Clean shaven. Classically handsome. Shaved head. Built like a football player."

So far, so good. "Smart?"

"Very. And charming." Iris smiled.

"Sounds perfect." Almost too good to be true. She wiped the sweat from her eyes. *What's wrong with him?*

"Ty's cousin would be, too. But he's recovering from his breakup."

"I remember." Rose felt an empathetic tug in her heart. "You told me."

"I don't think your plan would work if both of you brought baggage to it."

"I agree."

Two male joggers were advancing toward them. They had the long, lean, well-muscled look of professional athletes or narcissistic gym rats. Their naked torsos glistened with sweat like a neon sign flashing, Warning: Heartbreak Ahead. They caught Rose's gaze. Their confident smiles seemed to ask, "Do you like what you see?" Rose's scowl answered, "No, go jump in a lake." The men looked away. *Wise move, boys.*

"Maybe Lil knows someone, too." Iris's suggestion redirected Rose's attention.

"Can't ask Lil." They reached the end of their path. Rose turned as they jogged back to their cars. "She thinks I should go to the reunion alone. Ben would love that."

How could she possibly go to her law school reunion alone while Benjamin attended with his *pregnant* wife? The idea made her want to throw up. Benjamin would think she hadn't gotten over him. She wouldn't let him believe that.

Rose glanced toward Iris, who'd fallen silent beside her. She took a deep breath. "I'd like to meet Van."

Iris nodded. "Great. I'll set it up."

"Lunch next week?" Rose heard the tension in her voice.

"Why rush?"

Rose shrugged her shoulders. They'd just passed the high school and were heading back to the incline. She hated hills. "The sooner I meet Van." She paused to breathe again. "The sooner I'll know. Whether I need to find someone else."

Iris chuckled softly. "I think you'll agree. Van is perfect. For the role."

"Hope so." The stakes were high. The risks were steep. She'd already committed to this plan. She couldn't back out. Rose had to convince Benjamin and her former class-mates that she hadn't given him a moment's thought since she'd broken up with the lying, cheating snake almost two years ago.

Rose's shoulders slumped. Why did she have the feeling she was casting the role of a lifetime?

Donovan hadn't realized he'd had expecta-tions when he'd accepted Tyler's invitation to have lunch with him, Iris and her sister, the lawyer. But he was disappointed by the quiet, aloof woman Iris introduced as Rose. It was an appropriate name for someone who seemed covered in thorns. Donovan had assumed Iris's sister would be as warm and personable as Iris. He tried again to engage her in conversation.

"Where did you go to law school, Rose?" Donovan pitched his voice to be heard above the chatter from the surrounding tables in the crowded neighborhood restau-rant.

"University of Michigan." Her brief glance was dismissive. She returned her attention to her salmon salad.

"That surprises me." The spicy scent of his chicken parmesan lured Donovan back to his own entrée.

"Why?" Rose's head snapped up at Don-

31

ovan's comment. "Do you think I wouldn't be able to get into such a highly ranked law school?"

"Rose, I'm sure that wasn't what Van meant." Iris stared at her older sister beside her. She sounded surprised by Rose's reaction.

"That's not what I meant." Donovan was relieved to know Rose wasn't always this prickly. What had caused her uncharacteristic response? "Iris told me you and your sisters were born and raised in Columbus, home of The Ohio State University. I'm surprised you'd go to OSU's rival school."

Rose looked down her nose from the other side of the table. "I wasn't concerned about their rivalry. The University of Michigan has a good law school."

Tyler lowered his glass of iced tea. "Xavier and I were born in Columbus, too. But we chose to go out of state for college. That's where we met Van."

Rose nodded as though she was filing away the information on how he'd met the Anderson cousins.

Donovan heard the note of caution in Tyler's voice as his friend and coworker waded into the conversation. Perhaps Tyler also was caught off guard by Rose's behavior during this lunch. He'd thought Tyler had

32

met Iris's two sisters. Did Rose seem different from the first time he'd met her?

Maybe Donovan should stop while he was ahead. He couldn't imagine Rose agreeing to help the shelter pro bono. She didn't appear to be a very compassionate person. But he couldn't convince himself to leave the lawyer alone. He needed legal assistance to speak for his clients and their families. Besides, something about her chilly, judgmental demeanor challenged him, and Donovan had always been attracted to challenges.

"Are you saying you're not a Buckeye fan?" Donovan allowed his gaze to roam over Rose's face.

She was lovely. Her skin looked as smooth and warm as honey. Her elegant features were perfect: winged ebony eyebrows, a long, narrow nose, high cheekbones, a pointed chin. Her cocoa-brown eyes were wide and curious and framed by long, thick lashes. Her full, pink lips were classically curved. Such lips were meant for smiling. And kissing.

"I don't like college sports. I prefer the pros." Rose pinned him with a stare. "What about you?"

Would she grade me on my answer? "I like all sports, college and pros. Which teams do you like?"

"The Ohio ones, of course." She shrugged one slender, sexy shoulder. "I just wish they were better."

Rose earned points for supporting her home teams despite the fact that it had been longer than a while since any of Ohio's professional franchises had sniffed a championship. It took a lot of perseverance to stick with a team through its darkest seasons. But her chilly personality left her with a scoring deficit because she didn't seem approachable. Regret settled on his shoulders like a coat. Rose couldn't provide the legal representation they needed. He wanted someone who cared about the people, not just the process.

Now that he knew he wouldn't be working with her to represent the shelter and its clients, there was no reason for them to see each other again. Was there?

Rose considered Donovan in her peripheral vision. Iris had been wrong. Donovan wasn't right for the role of her fake boyfriend at all. Yes, he was successful and intelligent. But he was too charming. If he attended her reunion, he'd cast a spell over half of the attendees, if not all of them. And he was far too attractive. Rose glanced at him again. Contrary to popular opinion, she believed there was, in fact, such a thing as "too handsome." And Donovan Carroll fit that description. To perfection. So did Tyler. Judging from the attention the two received from the women at the other tables, Rose's theory had support. Did Iris notice the stares directed toward their table? How could she not?

Rose took another peek at Donovan. His shaved head was the sexiest thing she'd ever seen. His classically handsome sienna features were hypnotizing. She enjoyed watching his long, elegant hands move. And his bright, hazel eyes made her think wicked thoughts.

No, he wasn't a good choice for the role he'd unknowingly been auditioning for. Rose had known that the moment she'd seen him walk into the restaurant with Iris and Tyler. Their fake relationship would be blown the minute they showed up at the reunion. She'd have to keep track of the hotel room keys he'd be collecting. She didn't have time for that. But even with that realization, Rose couldn't stop auditioning him.

Donovan had settled back onto his seat beside Tyler in the booth. He was staring at his half-empty glass of iced tea as though it held the key to his future.

Rose took a sip of her ice water. "Your office must be very busy preparing for the launch of your latest computer game."

Iris had told Rose more than she needed to know about Anderson Adventures' upcoming release, Osiris' Journey, but it had been wonderful seeing her sister so excited and engaged in the project. It had been the happiest she'd seen Iris in years.

Donovan looked up from his drink. "Iris has done an excellent job with the product launch. Anderson Adventures is breaking all sorts of preorder records with Osiris' Journey."

"Thank you for the kind words, Van." Iris inclined her head. "But I think the preorders are a reflection of the product, not my work."

Rose glowed as though Donovan's compliment was meant for her. "Iris is fearless, in addition to being very talented and creative. She's going to go far. And so will Anderson Adventures, if you stick with her."

Iris's cheeks grew pink. "Rosie, Anderson Adventures is already very successful."

Rose swept a dismissive hand. "Imagine how much more successful they'll be with you on their team." She tilted her head. "Are you blushing?"

"I think she is." Tyler chuckled. He reached across the table and covered Iris's hand with his own. "You've given us the best product launch we've ever had. And you've helped us establish processes that will continue to grow our customer base."

Rose lowered her eyes to Iris and Tyler's joined hands. The genuine caring and affection in that gesture filled Rose with joy for her sister — as well as envy. She looked up, and her eyes were caught by Donovan's bright, hazel gaze.

She cleared her throat. "So what's next for Anderson Adventures?"

"We're working on future releases and our fall catalog." Donovan straightened.

"We're also planning a release party with Iris's help." Tyler looked to Rose. "You and Lily should join us."

"Oh, no." Rose swung her wide-eyed gaze from Tyler to Donovan. "We wouldn't want to intrude."

"It's not an intrusion," Tyler assured her. "Families are welcome. And we're bringing back the disc jockey from the internal associates launch."

"She was a big hit." Iris grinned. "You and Lily should come. You'd have a great time. I'm planning the party so I should know."

Rose laughed. "All right, you've convinced

me. But I want to be there when you invite Lily."

She looked again at Donovan. Her grin faded as she found his attention fixed on her mouth. The glint in his eyes caused her pulse to trip. His bright gaze lifted to hers. She caught her breath. What was happening? What was he thinking? Donovan blinked, and the moment was gone. *What a relief.*

Rose lifted her water glass to her lips. Her hand shook just slightly. Now that she'd ruled out the charismatic sales executive for the role of her fake boyfriend, there wasn't any reason for them to see each other again. Was there?

"What did you think?" Tyler followed Donovan into his office after lunch.

Tread carefully. We're talking about Ty's girlfriend's sister. Donovan thought highly of Iris, not only for her professional expertise, but also because she made Tyler happy.

"Thanks for introducing me to Rose." Donovan circled his desk and sank onto the black leather executive chair behind it. "But I don't think she'd be interested in this project."

Tyler lowered himself onto one of the gray visitor's chairs in front of Donovan's desk.

"Rose was a little . . ."

"Aloof?"

"Yes, but she wasn't like that the first time I met her."

"I'd wondered about that."

"And Iris loves her. She, Rose and Lily are very close. And a lot alike."

Donovan had wondered about that, too. But why had she been so cold and abrupt during lunch? "Did you tell her that I needed a lawyer?"

"No." Tyler's response was swift and definite. "I never mentioned it. I didn't think you'd want me to."

"I didn't." Donovan rubbed his forehead with his right hand. *What should I do now?* "I'd hoped to at least tell Rose about the shelter's situation, but she doesn't seem very approachable."

"Do you want me or Iris to speak with her?"

Donovan was shaking his head before Tyler finished his thought. "I don't want to put either of you in the middle. This is my problem."

"When are you going to understand that when one of us has a problem, we all have a problem?" Tyler's frown was chastising. "That's the way family works."

"You know it's hard for me to accept

help." Donovan restrained himself from squirming on his seat.

"This isn't for you. It's for the shelter's clients, the families you're trying to support."

"You're right." The truth in Tyler's words brought Donovan up short. "But I'll be the one to talk with Rose." *If* he decided it wouldn't be a waste of time.

Tyler spread his hands. "There's no harm in asking her, Van."

"So I've heard." He'd always hated that saying. "I may be asking too much, though. I need an experienced lawyer who cares about the case, but I also need someone who's willing to work for free."

"It's for an important cause."

Donovan swung his seat to better contemplate the cerulean, cloudless sky from his office window. Summer finally had landed in Columbus. They'd had a long and difficult winter, followed by a petulant spring. Although born and raised in Chicago — a much colder city — Donovan had lived in Columbus long enough to breathe a sigh of relief when the first rays of summer brought warmer temperatures.

"Most of the board supports filing the statement against allowing the pawnshop to move into our neighborhood. But a few members don't." Donovan spun his chair to face Tyler. "It's hard keeping the board together and focused on the plan. I'd like a lawyer who's sympathetic to our position so that I'm not pulling both the board and the lawyer."

"With great power comes great responsibility." Tyler quoted the line from Marvel Comics' *Spider-Man.*

Donovan gave a half smile at the reminder. "The other board members are looking for lawyers, too." Although Donovan suspected they weren't having any better luck than he was. No one had called him with recommendations. He swallowed another sigh.

Tyler checked his bronze wristwatch. "I thought you said your response was due next month? Today's June 22. You're running out of time."

And options. "I know. If we don't find a lawyer who'll work with us pro bono, I'll propose that the board members pool our money to pay a lawyer."

"How do you think that will go over?" Tyler arched a skeptical brow.

"Not well. It's also a poor precedent to set."

"If I were you, I'd talk with Whitley before suggesting the board split the bill." Tyler stood to leave.

"You're probably right." The thought of asking his ex-girlfriend for a favor turned his stomach.

As Tyler left his office, Donovan's thoughts returned to Rose. She would be a far better option than Whitley, but he'd have to offer her a proposal she couldn't refuse.

"What did you think?" Iris skipped the more formal greeting when Rose answered her office phone later that afternoon.

Tread carefully. Rose sat at her desk at the law firm of Apple & Spencer LLC. She'd been dreading Iris's call. She didn't want to offend her sister, but Iris had been wrong. Donovan wasn't fake boyfriend material.

"Van seems like a very nice person." Rose looked away from the documents she was reviewing on her computer screen. "But I don't think he's the right man for this plan."

There was a moment's surprised silence before Iris responded. "Are you kidding me? Why not?"

"He's a player."

"No, he's not."

"Are *you* kidding *me*?" Rose's eyebrows jumped toward her hairline. "It's in his eyes. It's in his smile. He's just too charming."

"Rosie, not every good-looking guy is a player." Iris's tone was gentle. "They're not all like Ben."

"I know." Rose squeezed her eyes shut. Consciously, she knew that, but subconsciously, she was still suspicious. "I don't want to take that risk."

"What risk?"

Rose opened her eyes. Her attention landed on the black metal inbox on the far corner of her cognac cherrywood desk. She'd emptied her inbox when she'd arrived early this morning. When she'd returned from lunch, it was full again. Her black wire organizer on the opposite end of her desk already was stuffed with project folders. Her cases and workload were multiplying like rabbits.

"Flirting is second nature to men like Van. They probably don't even realize they're doing it. If I took him to the reunion, he wouldn't be able to stop himself from flirting with other women." Rose rubbed her shoulder. Her gaze drifted to the matching cognac cherrywood bookcase on her left. It was swollen with reference books. Her certificates and awards hung nearby on the eggshell office walls.

"Van isn't like that." Iris's voice was adamant. "He's one of the good guys."

"You've only known him for three months. Ben fooled me for two years."

"Ty has known Van for seventeen years."

Rose froze. "Did you tell Ty that I wanted to check out Van as a possible date for my reunion?"

"Of course not." Iris seemed insulted by the question. "I'd never do that to you. And I'd slap you if you did something like that to me."

"I'm sorry. I didn't mean to offend you." Rose rubbed her right shoulder, trying to ease the tension building there.

"It's all right." Iris sighed. "Well, if Van's off your list, do you want to meet Xavier?"

"No, thank you." Xavier had just broken up with his girlfriend. This probably wasn't a good time to ask him to pretend to be in love with her.

"Then what are you going to do?"

I wish I knew. "I guess I'll have to ask Lil if she could recommend someone."

"Good luck getting Lily to cooperate with your plan. Do you think she even knows anyone who fits your criteria?" Iris sounded dubious.

"I don't know." Rose frowned. "But I'm desperate."

Lily would probably once again try to talk Rose into going to the reunion alone. That was something Rose was not going to do. She'd rather go to the reunion with Donovan "Heartthrob" Carroll than face Benjamin without a date. Unbidden, an image of Donovan came to mind. At least she'd have someone good to look at for the weekend.

CHAPTER 3

CHAPTER 3

"I can't stay long, but I did want to ask you for a favor." Rose smiled as Lily closed the door behind her Monday evening. Rose had called her sister as soon as she'd rung off with Iris that afternoon to ask if she could come by Lily's house after work.

"If I can, I'd be happy to help you. You know that." Lily kicked off her shoes before leading Rose down the hallway to her living room.

Rose took off her shoes and followed. She sank onto the powder blue love seat as Lily settled onto the near corner of the matching sofa.

"I found out Friday that Ben's wife is pregnant." Rose had given her explanation a lot of consideration on her forty-five-minute drive to Lily's house.

"Oh, Rose. I'm so sorry." Concern darkened Lily's whiskey eyes. "I can understand how that would hurt."

"Thank you." Rose had never been comfortable expressing her feelings, but Lily's caring made it easier. "I'd been uncomfortable about going to my reunion when I thought it was going to be just Ben and his wife. Now that I know his wife is pregnant, I'm even more uneasy."

"What do you have to be uncomfortable about?" Lily tilted her head. "You're not the one who was cheating on your fiancée for two years. Ben and his wife should be the ones who are uncomfortable."

"I agree with what you're saying, logically. But you know feelings aren't always logical." Rose wished she was more like Lily, calm and rational.

"I know." Lily inclined her head, the image of grace and serenity. "That's why we have to think before we act so we aren't impulsive. That's what you're always telling Iris."

Iris, the impetuous one.

Restless and impatient, Rose stood from the love seat to pace the living room. Her stocking feet sank into the plush, violet carpeting that Lily had had installed last year.

"I *have* thought about it, Lil." Rose crossed from the love seat to the fireplace. "I've given it a lot of rational consideration, and I've decided that I want to hurt Ben. A lot."

"I understand." Lily's voice carried from behind Rose, where she remained on the sofa. "When Ben hurt you, I wanted to hurt him a lot, too. But you're going about it the wrong way."

"You think the right way is going to the reunion alone?" Rose turned toward her sister. Irritation flooded her veins like an electrical current. "I'm after revenge, not a higher level of enlightenment."

"How will showing up at the reunion with a fake date avenge you?" Lily's voice was frustratingly calm.

"Not just any fake date — someone who's more attractive, successful and intelligent than Ben." *Someone like Donovan,* her mind whispered. Rose shook her head to banish the voice.

"But he'd be a fake. That doesn't prove that you're over Ben. That just proves that you're creative."

Rose didn't appreciate her sister's attempt at humor. "The Constant Classmates are pitying me. I don't want to get the same looks and comments from the rest of my class."

Lily shifted forward on the sofa. "Rosie, if you pander to other people's reactions and judgments, you'll exhaust yourself. Don't follow other people. Be yourself."

"I *am* being myself." Rose paced away from the fireplace and back to the love seat. "It's *my* own idea to get a fake fiancé."

"Can you even hear yourself?" Lily seemed part amused, part frustrated. "You're going to be yourself by doing something fake. That doesn't make sense."

"Not to you because you're a confident person." Rose leaned forward, resting her forearms on her knees and linking her fingers together. "I used to be confident, too. Ben took that from me."

"Then take it back." Lily ran her fingers through her wavy, shoulder-length hair. Her movements were graceful. "I know Ben shook your self-confidence. Do you think it's easy for me to see you like this?"

"I'd feel better if I could get even."

"You're giving Ben too much power."

Rose expelled an impatient breath. She rubbed the knotted muscles in her right shoulder. "Lil, are you going to help me or not?"

Lily frowned her confusion. "What can *I* do?"

Rose hesitated. "Do you know any eligible men who might be willing to be my date for the reunion?"

Lily seemed to consider the question. Rose appreciated that. At least she didn't dismiss Rose's request immediately.

"No, I'm afraid I don't." Lily offered a smile. "The men I know are either in relationships or you don't have to ask why they aren't."

"It sounds like we know a lot of the same men." Rose's tone was wry.

"Have you asked Iris?"

"She doesn't know anyone suitable." Donovan's image taunted Rose.

Lily nodded. "You and I disagree on this fake date idea, but in the end I just want you to be happy. I want you to be Rosie again."

Rose wanted the same thing. She wanted to get rid of this bitterness, anger and jealousy, and move on with her life. But how could she do that? What was the first step back to herself?

Donovan didn't want to have this conversation again. However, it seemed that Cecil Lowell, the newest member of the Hope Homeless Shelter's board of directors and the most junior member of the five-person legal subcommittee, didn't have anything better to do.

"We already voted on this motion last

week." Donovan regarded the young banker. He drew a deep breath to hold on to his patience. The conference room in the shelter's offices smelled as old and musty as the rest of the building.

The subcommittee had voted during its previous meeting, and presented their decision and reasoning to the entire board of directors. Now with the board's support, they were preparing to move forward with their challenge to allowing a pawnshop to move into Hope Homeless Shelter's neighborhood. Why did Cecil want to revisit that near-unanimous decision? Was it because he had been the only nay vote?

Donovan sat at the head of the honeywood conference table. The other four subcommittee members — two women and two men — were on either side of the small, rectangular table. Cecil was on his immediate right.

"I know." The flush on Cecil's round cheeks almost matched his curly red hair. "But I've thought of some other things that we need to consider."

"Like what?" Kim Lee, seated across from Cecil, had served on the board longer than Donovan. The retired university professor glanced at her silver watch. It was the only sign of her impatience.

"The reason we need a lawyer pro bono is because the shelter's low on dollars." Cecil glanced around the table as he spoke.

"That's *one* of the reasons." Salma Vargas propped her elbow on the table and balanced her pointed chin in the palm of her hand. The certified public accountant eyed Cecil with vague curiosity.

Cecil continued as though Salma hadn't spoken. "If the city allows Public Pawn to open in our neighborhood, the owners could be persuaded to become regular donors. They could increase our fundraising base."

"You said you had something new to add," Kim said, crossing her arms over her dark green blouse. "You said basically the same thing last week."

Cecil shook his head. "I hadn't suggested how we could use the extra money."

"Your new proposal is that we ask the pawnshop owners to make regular contributions to the homeless shelters. Is that correct?" Medgar Lawrence's brown eyes focused on Cecil seated beside him.

"Exactly." Cecil seemed excited that someone understood his plan.

"I don't think supporting homeless shelters is Public Pawn's primary mission." A few more creases lined Medgar's dark, weathered brow as his frown deepened.

"We could at least ask them. There's no harm in asking." Cecil leaned forward on his seat.

"Medgar is right." Donovan nodded his understanding of Medgar's point. "Cecil, these are two separate issues. If Public Pawn's owners wanted to support the shelter, they would already be donors. The other issue is that this committee has already voted to oppose the pawnshop locating here."

Cecil glanced between Donovan and Medgar. "You don't understand —"

"No, Cecil, you're the one who's confused." Donovan turned to the younger man. "The subcommittee voted on this matter *last* Wednesday and presented our position to the board, who approved our decision. Now we're moving forward."

"All right." Cecil threw up his hands. "I thought you'd want to hear different ideas."

"We heard different ideas *last* Wednesday." Donovan spoke slowly and clearly. "Now it's time to act."

"I agree. What's our next step?"

Donovan inclined his head toward the accountant, acknowledging her support. "We need to find a lawyer who'll take the case pro bono. I can't stress that enough. The shelter doesn't have the money for legal representation."

Kim glanced around the table. "But we need someone who's experienced with filing statements with the city."

"I've already checked with a couple." Medgar shook his head. "Neither one was interested. They said it was too many hours not to get paid. And a lot of those hours are spent following up with the city."

"Can we offer some nominal fee?" Salma asked. "Maybe we could at least get a deep discount."

Donovan looked around the table. "If it comes to that, we'll see if someone will take the case for a modest fee."

"A very modest fee." Medgar held Donovan's gaze. "If we sneeze in the wrong direction, our budget will end up in the red."

Donovan pushed away from the conference table. "And remember, everyone, the clock's still ticking. We need to find help fast."

Donovan winced after his first sip of coffee Friday morning. He turned to Tyler, seated beside him in front of Xavier's desk. "You call this coffee? Why bother?"

Tyler cradled his twenty-ounce, silver-and-black coffee mug between his palms like a day-old baby. "This is actually the way most humans drink coffee. We don't usually use it to peel off the soles of our shoes."

Donovan scowled into his coffee mug. He really could have used something stronger this morning. Worry about the shelter had kept him from sleeping, but unfortunately, he hadn't gotten to the office early enough to make the first pot of java.

Xavier gave him a considering look. "How was your conversation with Whitley last night?"

Donovan drank more of the warm water masquerading as coffee. What were the chances it would taste better if he just added more grounds? "She's not interested in the project."

Although she had made it quite clear that she was interested in a physical relationship with him. If he'd been eighteen, he might have accepted her offer. Whitley Maxwell was a beautiful woman. At one point, he'd considered spending the rest of his life with her. But at thirty-six, Donovan was done playing games. He was looking for some-thing more serious.

Tyler set his right ankle on his left knee. "I'm sorry things didn't work out."

"So am I." Today was June 26. They had two weeks left to file a statement with the city council. Donovan could almost hear the clock ticking. It had kept him up late last night and driven him out of his house early this morning.

"This confirms you were right to break off with Whitley in the first place." Xavier sat back on his executive chair.

"She broke off with me, remember?" Donovan rubbed his forehead. "But now I'm officially out of options for legal representation. None of the other board members have found someone willing to represent us for free, either."

Tyler cocked his head. "You're not completely out of options."

"You're talking about Rose."

"You haven't even asked her if she'd be interested in your case." Tyler gestured toward Donovan with his mug. "You're basing your decision on your first impression, which I admit was not great."

"Did she come across as that bad?" Xavier looked from Tyler to Donovan.

"Yes, she did." Donovan sighed. "But I was thinking of calling her later today. As Ty said, there's no harm in asking." He didn't feel any more optimistic about asking Rose than he'd felt asking Whitley.

"Good luck." Xavier saluted him with his coffee mug.

"I'll need it." Donovan looked to Tyler. "Do you have any suggestions on how to approach Rose?"

"Let her know how important this filing is to you and how many lives would be impacted."

Xavier inclined his head. "That's good advice. You may also want to let her know what's in it for her."

Donovan gave his friend a puzzled look. "Which would be what?"

Xavier grinned. "Having you in her debt."

"Very funny." Donovan stood to leave. But Xavier's comment raised an interesting question. If Rose did this favor for him, what would she want in return? And would he be willing to cut a deal?

Later Friday morning, Donovan's phone rang. Apple & Spencer LLC appeared in his caller identification display. Donovan stared at his phone in disbelief. How could one of the most prestigious law firms in the city have his direct phone number, and why were they calling him? Had someone on the board's legal subcommittee reached out to Apple & Spencer about their situation?

He tamped down his excitement and grabbed the receiver by the third ring. "Donovan Carroll." Silence met his greeting. "Hello?"

"Van, this is Rose Beharie. I know this is short notice but I wondered if you were free this evening? I'd like to discuss a, um, business proposal with you." Her voice poured over the phone like warm Scotch. It took him a moment to focus on her words.

"I wasn't expecting to hear from you." Was he hallucinating?

"Am I calling at a bad time?"

It was never a bad time to listen to a voice like hers. The soft, smooth tone made him think of silken sheets and turned-down lights. A little Teddy Pendergrass music playing softly in the background.

Donovan gave himself a mental shake. "No, this isn't a bad time at all. It's good to hear from you." He winced. He'd sounded stupid.

"I'm glad that you think so." Rose chuckled. The sound caused the muscles in his lower abdomen to dance.

Donovan pictured her as he'd last seen her in the restaurant. Her dark red blouse had made the honeyed tones of her skin glow. Her pencil-straight, knee-length skirt had hugged her slim hips. But her aloof demeanor had distracted him from her grade A, sexy voice. "You said something about a business proposal."

58

"That's right." She hesitated. "Are you available to meet with me after work today? Perhaps I could buy you a cup of coffee."

This was perfect. Donovan had been intending to call Rose later this morning, but he hadn't figured out how to get the conversation started. Now she'd called him. He imagined himself pumping his fist in victory. He wasn't out of the woods yet, though. He stared blindly across his office while his mind spun with questions. "What kind of business proposal do you have in mind?"

"I'd rather not go into the details over the phone."

Now he was really curious. "Could you give me a hint?"

She gave him another sample of her sexy chuckle instead. "I promise that it's nothing illegal or morally compromising. It's nothing that would show you or Anderson Adventures in a poor light."

"I hadn't imagined it would be."

"Then you'll meet with me this evening after work?"

"Yes, I will." In fact, he was looking forward to it, perhaps more than he should be.

They took a few minutes to select a time and place. They settled on a downtown coffee shop at six o'clock.

"I appreciate your agreeing to meet with me on such short notice, Van."

Donovan frowned. Rose still sounded uncertain. Should he be concerned? What was this business proposition, and why did she seem unsure as to whether she wanted to involve him?

"You're welcome. I'll see you later."

They ended their conversation. Donovan recradled his phone, then sat back on his chair. This was an interesting development. Finally, something good had happened. He was cautiously optimistic about the evening ahead. What was her business proposal and how could he use it to his advantage?

When Donovan entered the little coffee shop near downtown Columbus Friday night, Rose experienced the same reaction she'd had the first time they'd met. Her heart bounced. Her breath stuck in her throat. Her skin heated. That afternoon at lunch with Iris, Tyler and Donovan, she'd thought her reaction was just nerves. Was it nerves again tonight?

Her wave caught his attention and his half smile trapped her breath again. He moved with the fluid grace of a natural athlete. He was so deliciously tall and wickedly fit. Did

60

he know his forest green jersey molded to his chiseled biceps and his cocoa slacks hinted at the strength of his thighs? She imagined Benjamin gnashing his teeth in envy and smiled.

Once again, Rose was left to wonder why a strikingly handsome, dangerously sexy, successful, intelligent man was free on such short notice on a Friday night. There must have been someone in his little black book that he could have hooked up with.

"Have you been waiting long?" Donovan folded his long, lean body onto the seat on the other side of the small circular table. He sounded concerned.

"I was early. Nerves, I guess." Rose could have pulled her tongue right out of her head. *Why did I say that?*

"Sounds like you could use a cup of coffee." Donovan's hazel eyes were bright with curiosity, but he didn't push. Rose appreciated that.

She led the way to the customer counter, aware of Donovan's presence close behind her. At the cash register, Rose ordered two cups of coffee.

Donovan placed his hand on her forearm. "I can get it."

Rose tilted her head back to meet his eyes. He was a bit taller than Benjamin. That was

61

another point in his favor. "I invited you. I should pay."

A stubborn light flashed across his bright eyes before he dropped his hand from her arm. "I'll get the next one."

Rose smiled. He already envisioned them sharing coffee a second time. That was a good sign, wasn't it?

At the coffee station, Rose filled her mug, then doctored her coffee with cream and sweetener. Donovan drank his coffee black and sweet. They returned to the table. Fortunately, no one else had taken it.

"Thank you again for meeting me this evening." Rose reclaimed her seat.

"I was curious about this business proposition you mentioned." Donovan angled his chair to sit with his long legs away from the table.

She still wasn't sure how best to ease into her request. "It's actually a bit of a long story."

Donovan shrugged his remarkably broad shoulders. "I don't have any plans for the night."

Why was that?

"My law school class's ten-year reunion is this September. It's actually September eighteenth through the twentieth. I need an escort."

"An escort?" Donovan's almond-shaped eyes held her gaze as though he could read her mind and separate truth from fiction.

Rose took a deep breath, drawing in the scent of every item on the café's menu. "I need someone to pretend to be my boyfriend for the weekend."

Donovan blinked. He was silent for too many seconds. "Are you asking *me* to do that?"

"Yes." Rose's voice was thin, the word barely audible. She straightened her shoulders and tried again. "Yes, I am."

Again Donovan was silent. "There's got to be a story in there somewhere."

"That's not important."

"I think it is. If you want me to play this part for you — for an entire weekend — I need to know what I'm walking into."

Rose gave Donovan her best prosecutorial stare. The sales executive held her gaze while he sipped his coffee. He wasn't backing down. Rose smothered a groan. What could she tell him?

"All right." Rose heaved a sigh. She took a drink of her cooling coffee, then told him just enough. "My ex-fiancé and his newly pregnant wife will be at the reunion."

"So?" Donovan shrugged again.

Rose followed the movement, fascinated

by the play of muscles beneath the dark jersey. "So we didn't part on the best terms, and I'd rather he didn't know that I'm not dating."

"How long ago did you break up with this guy?"

"Why does that matter?"

"I'd like to know the circumstances that I'll be walking into."

Rose gritted her teeth. She hadn't counted on having to reveal so much of her background to a virtual stranger. "It's been almost a year and a half."

Donovan's thick, dark eyebrows jumped up his broad forehead. "And you haven't dated anyone else in all that time?"

Rose's temper started a slow burn. "Are you willing to help me or not?"

He cocked his head as though giving it some thought. "Why did you break up?"

"That doesn't matter."

"I'm sorry, but I think it does. It will help me to understand how you'll react when you see this guy. What's his name?"

"Ben Shippley."

"Why did you and Ben break up?"

He was persistent. Rose usually admired that quality in a person; not this time.

"Our values were too different. We didn't want the same things." She wanted monogamy; Benjamin did not. "And those are the only questions I'm going to answer for you. Are you willing to help me or not?"

Donovan stared into her eyes as though once again trying to read her mind. Rose held his intense gaze — and her breath. What would she do if Donovan turned her down? She wasn't going to her reunion with a perfect stranger. And the registrations were due next week. If she were going to decline to attend, it was now or never. But she didn't want to back out. She didn't want Benjamin to even consider that her absence had anything to do with him, the snake.

"All right." Donovan broke the tense silence. "I'll accompany you to your reunion as your boyfriend —"

Rose's features relaxed into a smile of relief. "Thank you —"

Donovan held out his left hand, palm out, to stop her. "But I want something in return."

CHAPTER 4

Donovan examined Rose's expression. How quickly she'd gone from jubilant relief to wary distrust. Seconds ago, she'd glowed with happiness. She'd smiled and his motor skills had leaked from his brain. Her elegant features were just so beautiful. Her wide cocoa gaze mesmerized him. A man could lose himself — or find himself — in her eyes.

Rose was a beautiful, intelligent, fascinating woman. Donovan felt sorry for Benjamin Shippley. He must have been devastated when Rose broke up with him. *Was Shippley's loss my gain?*

"I need a lawyer." He hadn't meant to be so blunt, but there it was.

Rose lowered her porcelain mug to the table. Her eyes examined his features. "What kind of trouble are you in?"

Donovan's lips tilted in a half smile. Tyler and Xavier had made the same assumption. "Do you always presume the worst?"

Rose arched a brow. Donovan had an inexplicable urge to trace its winged path. He clenched both hands around his still-warm mug.

"Usually people only need a lawyer when they're in trouble." Rose lifted her mug to her lips again.

"Then you're right. I need help with a problem."

"What kind of problem?"

Donovan glanced around the small coffee shop. The clientele were starting to change. Young men and women who were interested in doing more than drinking coffee on a Friday night were clearing out. Older couples wandered in from their nearby homes, looking for a quiet way to entertain themselves and an after-dinner snack they didn't have to prepare. The air was strong with the scent of flavored coffee beans and fresh-baked pastries. The rumble of conversation ebbed and flowed, spiked now and again with gales of laughter.

He returned his attention to Rose. "I'm president of the Hope Homeless Shelter's board of directors. We recently received confirmation from the city council that they're considering permitting a pawnshop to open on the same block as one of our homeless shelters."

"Are you opposed to having the pawnshop in your neighborhood?"

"Yes, we are."

"Why?" Rose had a great poker face. Did they teach that in law school?

Donovan couldn't tell from her tone or expression whether she agreed with his board's position. The uncertainty was unsettling. "Studies have shown a link between increased crime and pawnshops. Our board has voted to file a statement with the city council explaining our opposition to the pawnshop's location."

"And you want my help to file this statement."

"Yes." Donovan hesitated. "There's just one problem. Our budget is very restrictive. We don't have the money to pay for legal services."

"You want me to work pro bono." Rose spoke without inflection. Her expression was sphinx-like.

Donovan tried to read her eyes. What was her reaction to his request? "We're operating on a very tight budget. We hadn't anticipated the need for extensive legal services." It was a true statement. Still, he wasn't comfortable making the excuses.

"Filing a legal statement is a lot of work. I can't just sit down at a computer and whip something up."

Donovan still couldn't read her reaction. Was she going to say no? Her refusal would have consequences, though. "I realize a legal brief isn't a quick and easy document. Your reunion lasts an entire weekend."

Rose's eyes narrowed. "Are you comparing writing a statement to a reunion weekend?"

"You're asking me to give up an entire weekend and spend it trying to convince strangers that we're in love." Donovan gestured toward her with his coffee mug. "You're an attractive woman, but that's still a lot to ask."

"It would be like a vacation for you."

Donovan leaned closer. "Some vacation, surrounded by strangers. Having my every move planned. And it'll be football season. Will the activities be scheduled around the NFL games?"

He thought he could see steam puffing from her ears. Rose leaned into the table. Donovan was briefly distracted by her scent, vanilla and cinnamon.

She lowered her voice. "I'll pay for our registration and hotel. All you'll have to do is show up."

Paying for his coffee was one thing; she was not paying for his registration or hotel.

"I'll be at your beck and call for two whole days, possibly longer. And you're requiring a great deal of acting skill." He faked an apologetic expression. "Like I said, you're a very attractive woman." Stunning, in fact. "But I don't know if there's any chemistry between us."

"Are you saying that if I don't write and submit this statement for you for free, you won't attend my reunion with me and pretend to be my boyfriend?" Rose's generous lips thinned as she glared at him.

"Consider it a fair trade." Donovan spread his hands.

They held each other's gaze for several silent moments. For Donovan, it wasn't a hardship. He kind of liked the way her wide cocoa eyes gleamed when she was irritated. His eyes traced the delicate curve of her clenched jawline and her small, stubborn chin.

"Fine." Rose broke the brief quiet with a huff. "You drive a hard bargain. But if you agree to attend my reunion as my devoted and love-struck boyfriend, I'll file your statement opposing the pawnshop's plan to locate in the Hope Homeless Shelter's neighborhood."

Rose extended her slender, elegant hand across the table. Donovan shook it. His much larger hand closed over her graceful fingers. The sensation of her skin, soft and warm against his, traveled up his arm and settled in his chest. He wasn't the only one who felt something — Rose stared at their joined hands, then lifted her gaze to his. She seemed surprised.

"I should be going." She tugged free of him. She reached into her purse as she stood. "Thank you again for meeting with me. Here's my card. Call me Monday, and we'll arrange to get together to discuss your brief."

"Rose." Donovan put a hand on her arm to detain her — and because he wanted to touch her again. "Thank you for agreeing to help us. This really does mean a lot to our clients and their families."

Rose nodded. "Have a good weekend." She dashed off before he could wish her the same.

Donovan watched over her until she disappeared from the coffee shop. Then he studied his hand. He could still feel her skin like warm silk against his palm. He closed his fist to hold on to the sensation a little longer. Why would a woman as beautiful, interesting and intelligent as Rose Beharie need a fake boyfriend?

■ ■ ■ ■

On Monday evening, Rose entered the fifth-floor offices of Anderson Adventures. Her black pumps were silent as she crossed the silver-and-black carpet toward the reception desk. The cool, comfortable decor seemed very understated for a multimillion-dollar company.

The nameplate of the attractive older woman seated behind the modern, modular front desk read Sherry Parks. She gave Rose a welcoming smile. "You must be Rose Beharie. You look so much like your sister."

"It's nice to meet you, Sherry." Rose offered the receptionist her hand. "My sister speaks very fondly of you."

Iris's description of Sherry had been spot-on. The older woman did resemble Doris Day with her pretty, wholesome features, blond bob and bright cornflower-blue eyes.

"Iris is a sweetheart. I miss seeing her every day." Sherry released Rose's hand. She picked up the telephone receiver and pressed a few buttons. "I'll let Van know you're here."

As Sherry told Van she'd arrived for their 5:30 p.m. meeting to discuss his statement, Rose settled onto one of the gray guest chairs. She idly scanned her surroundings as she stood her briefcase on the floor beside her and balanced her purse on her lap. Despite its cool glass-and-metal decor, the reception area gave the impression of warmth and welcome.

Sherry replaced the phone. "Van's on his way. Would you like some coffee?"

"I'd love some. Thank you." Although Iris had warned her about the size of Anderson Adventures' coffee mugs.

"Cream and sugar?" Sherry stood.

"Cream and sweetener, please."

"I'll be right back." Sherry walked past other administrative desks, then disappeared into a back room.

Rose returned to her scrutiny of the reception area. The latest industry magazines were arranged across a tempered glass Caravan desk in the far corner. Framed covers of the company's computer games were displayed on the eggshell walls. Interspersed with those images were candid photographs of happy employees, dating from decades earlier to present day.

"Here you are." Sherry returned, carrying the largest coffee mug Rose had ever seen.

"If I finish this, I won't sleep for the rest of the week." Rose was only half joking. The silver-and-black mug looked like it held twenty ounces of coffee, at least. Rose relieved Sherry of its weight.

"The Andersons are addicted to coffee." Sherry returned to her desk.

Rose considered the large mug. *How many of these minitubs of caffeine had Donovan consumed before meeting me for coffee Friday night?*

"Sorry to keep you waiting." Donovan's smooth baritone interrupted her thoughts.

"Not at all." Rose stood, balancing the mug in her right hand. "Sherry made me quite comfortable." She offered the receptionist a grateful smile.

Sherry's blue eyes twinkled as she collected her purse and tote bag. "It was a pleasure to meet you, Rose. Please tell Iris I said hello."

"I will." Rose adjusted her purse on her left shoulder and collected her briefcase.

Donovan cupped Rose's elbow to guide her down the hall, presumably toward his office. "Thanks, Sherry. Have a good evening."

"You, too, Van," Sherry called after them.

Rose walked beside Donovan past the frosted glass walls of the company's offices. The warmth of his hand on her elbow through the linen material of her sapphire-blue blazer made it difficult for Rose to collect her thoughts. She had to clear her mind. Focus on something else. She —

Rose stopped short in the threshold to Donovan's office. She'd glimpsed his name and title on the silver metal plate beside the door. Donovan stepped aside to let her enter before him. She wasn't certain she wanted to.

"Are we meeting in here?" She couldn't tear her eyes away from the scene in front of her.

"Yes." He had the nerve to sound confused.

Was he blind to the disaster zone that was his work area? The spacious office looked as though a paper mill — perhaps several paper mills — had vomited across every surface of every piece of furniture in the room. Folders and printouts were strewn across his desk. Magazines and newspapers grew on top of his circular conversation table. File folders sat on the chairs around it. The two bulletin boards mounted to the wall on her left were covered with memos. Some appeared to be three sheets deep. Binders stood on the silver carpet.

"How do you find anything in here?" Rose gingerly entered the room.

Donovan walked past her. He moved a stack of magazines from one of the gray cushioned chairs around his conversation table to the floor beside his desk. He then dug through the turmoil on the right corner of his desk and liberated two manila folders, each about a half inch thick.

"I have a system." He returned to the table with the folders.

"Prove it." Rose once again looked around in disbelief.

"Wasn't it Einstein who asked if a cluttered desk is the sign of a cluttered mind, what does an empty desk mean?"

"Einstein never met you."

Donovan's burst of laughter startled Rose. She'd insulted him but instead of being offended, Donovan was amused. His face was alive with humor. The rich, warm sound vibrated in Rose's lower abdomen.

"My first impression of you was wrong." Donovan's laughter ended, leaving a sexy grin in its place.

"What was it?" *Do I really want to know?*

"I thought you didn't have a sense of humor."

Is that the way I came across during our first meeting? Rose stiffened. Maybe Lily and Iris were right. She'd allowed her breakup with Benjamin to change her — and not for the better.

"I'm glad I could entertain you. But we'd

better get started on your submission statement." She settled onto one of the seats at the conversation table.

Donovan watched Rose cross her long, slender legs, visible beneath the hem of her conservative blue business dress. He chose the seat beside her. There was a chill in the air after the comment about her seeming humorless when they'd first met. He shouldn't have said that. He'd lost ground with the only lawyer who'd agreed to help the shelter.

He handed Rose one of the manila folders. "I made a copy of all of our project documents for you."

"Thank you." Rose removed a pen from her purse. She flipped open the folder, then skimmed the memos, press releases and letters contained within. With her pen, she underlined several phrases. "You've already shared a lot of communication with the city council members."

"Many of our clients are recovering addicts — drugs, alcohol or both. Most of them have been arrested and are going through a court-mandated rehabilitation program." Donovan tried but failed to read Rose's reaction to the information he'd given her. What did she think about the shelter's clients and the neighborhood in which they lived?

"Does the shelter provide this program?" Rose pinned him with a look. In her eyes, he recognized a brilliant, capable lawyer. But would she be sympathetic to their cause?

"We offer drug and alcohol rehabilitation, in addition to job-search and some training services." Donovan thought he saw a glint of admiration in her eyes. That was a good sign.

"How many clients do you have?" Rose returned her attention to the folder.

"That depends on the season. We average about one hundred men at Shelter West and about fifty women at Shelter East. The houses are next to each other."

"And your primary objection to the proposed pawnshop is the nature of the business itself." Rose's voice lacked inflection.

"Our clients are at a vulnerable stage of recovery. Having a pawnshop a block away from the shelter would be too great of a temptation for them. It would give them easy access to a means of getting money for drugs and alcohol."

"I see." Rose nodded, underlining something on a document.

"Do you agree with us?" Donovan

watched her closely.

"What I think doesn't matter. I don't have to agree with you to represent you."

"But I want to know what you think."

Rose hesitated. "As a member of the shelter's board of directors, you know your clients and their needs better than the city council does."

"But you don't agree with us."

"I understand your concern that the pawnshop would be a temptation to your clients." Rose finally looked at him. "But that neighborhood is in desperate need of economic investment. Having a business move into that community could only help."

"But we need the right business. And that's not a pawnshop." Donovan believed that with every fiber of his being. "We're trying to strengthen this community. To do that, we need businesses that would attract other businesses. Pawnshops would attract more crime."

"Most of them require valid photo identification to process transactions." Rose gestured toward him with her silver Cross Pen. "It's not in the best interest of pawnshop proprietors to deal in misappropriated property. Police regularly cross-check the stores' inventory against theft reports. If the store is caught with stolen items, the owner is penalized."

Her lawyer speak was turning him on. "It's not a coincidence that neighborhoods with pawnshops also have high rates of property crime."

"According to the National Pawnbrokers Association, less than one tenth of one percent of pawnshops deal in stolen goods." She shrugged a shoulder. "I've done my research."

"So have I." Donovan sat back on his chair. "It's not just my clients that I'm concerned about. I'm looking at the community as a whole. It's not just about the crime rate, which studies don't dispute, by the way. These are low-income families. The high interest rates these shops charge for their so-called loans take advantage of poor people. This community is a vulnerable population. We can't let them be further exploited."

Rose stared at him in silence so intently and for so long that Donovan forced himself not to squirm under her regard. "What's wrong?"

"Nothing." She shook her head as though waking from a daydream. "It's just . . . You could make me believe in heroes."

Donovan's face heated. He returned his attention to his folder. "I'm not a hero."

"Real heroes never see themselves that way." Rose's response was soft and low, almost inaudible.

He wasn't a hero. These families had fallen on hard times just as his family had when he was a child. He was just trying to pay back. That didn't make him a hero.

But the look in Rose's eyes made him believe he could be.

CHAPTER 5

"Why am I here?" Lily must have asked variations of that same question a dozen times since she'd learned she and her sisters had been invited to the celebration party for the launch of Anderson Adventures' latest computer game, Osiris' Journey.

Rose rolled her eyes as she entered the Columbus Convention Center with her sisters Friday night. It had been eleven days since she'd met with Donovan to work on the Hope Homeless Shelter's submission statement to the Columbus City Council. Since that initial face-to-face consultation, Rose had worked with Donovan via email to finalize the statement. She'd submitted it to city council that morning. It hadn't been as easy working out the details of the letter's language via email, but it had been less distracting. His handsome features hadn't tempted her, and his smooth baritone hadn't seduced her.

"You're here because you didn't want to embarrass me by declining Anderson Adventures' gracious invitation to the three of us." Iris delivered her explanation as patiently this twelfth time as she had the first time Lily had grumbled.

"It's not as though you had anything better to do." Rose followed Iris into the large ballroom reserved for the launch party. Her baby sister looked like a queen in her figure-hugging emerald dress.

Rose scanned the room. She told herself she wasn't searching for Donovan. If she repeated that statement often enough, she might eventually believe it. What would Donovan think of her formfitting black dress?

Why do I care?

"Actually, I did have plans for tonight." Lily's voice was barely audible above the pop song blaring through the speakers.

"What were they?" Rose was puzzled. Lily hadn't mentioned another appointment.

Her middle sister shook her head. "They aren't important."

Lily's response further piqued Rose's curiosity but she didn't push. She glanced at her sister's outfit. The high-waisted, magenta dress complemented Lily's warm gold complexion and highlighted her stunning figure. Not for the first time, Rose wished she had Lily's cleavage.

"You look beautiful." Rose squeezed her sister's hand.

Lily gave her a startled look. "Thank you. So do you."

"Thank you." Rose turned away to scan the room again. Iris had explained that, unlike the initial internal launch, for this celebration, Anderson Adventures' associates had been encouraged to bring a date. That explained why the large ballroom was packed. Rose finally spotted Donovan walking toward her with a smile that would sell a lot of toothpaste. Tyler was beside him, along with three other very attractive people. Were good looks a requirement for admittance to the computer gaming company's executive team?

"I'm glad you could make it." Donovan took her hand. His deep voice shot through her system like rum.

"Thank you for inviting me." Rose wrestled her gaze from Donovan's smiling hazel eyes.

Tyler wrapped an arm around Iris, tucking her against his side. "Can you make the introductions?"

"Of course." Iris gestured first to Rose. "My sisters, Rose and Lily Beharie." She then turned to the Anderson family. "You've met Ty. This is Foster Anderson, Ty's father and the company's chief executive officer."

Tyler had inherited his father's strikingly handsome features. Foster stepped forward to shake hands with Rose. "Soon to be the company's *retired* CEO. It's a pleasure to meet you, my dear."

Iris had explained to Rose and Lily that Foster was going to announce his retirement later this summer and turn the company's leadership over to Tyler.

Foster turned to greet Lily. "And it's a pleasure to see you again, Lily. I can't thank you enough for giving me Iris's business card."

Lily grinned as she shook Foster's hand. "It's wonderful to see you again, sir."

"Foster, please." Foster patted her shoulder.

Iris continued the introductions. "Kayla Cooper Anderson is a member of the executive board."

The older woman exuded timeless grace and style as she stepped forward to take Rose's and Lily's hands. Her large onyx eyes twinkled with satisfaction and perhaps mischief. "I've been anxious to meet Iris's sisters. You both look lovely. Thank you for coming."

"Thank you for having us." Rose returned Kayla's smile.

"It's a pleasure to meet you." Lily's tone was gracious. If Rose didn't know better, she'd think her sister was happy to be here.

"Rose and Van have already met." Iris interrupted the exchange. "Lily, this is Van Carroll. He's vice president of sales for Anderson Adventures." She paused as her middle sister greeted the sales executive. "And Xavier Anderson is the company's vice president of finance and Kayla's son."

Rose offered Tyler's cousin a warm smile, but inside she was hurting for him. She was aware that Xavier recently had been betrayed by his girlfriend. Rose knew how much such deception hurt.

"Nice to meet you." Xavier inclined his head as he shook her hand. Then he turned to Lily and his greeting seemed to linger. "Thank you for coming."

Lily returned his greeting without seeming to notice the intensity in Xavier's onyx eyes.

"We'd be honored if you'd join us at the lead table." Foster extended the invitation as he offered Kayla his left arm.

Tyler escorted Iris. Xavier gestured for Lily to precede him, which left Rose and Donovan to bring up the rear.

Rose racked her brain for something to say to break the awkward tension. "I submitted your statement this morning."

"Thank you." Donovan gave her his money smile.

Rose looked away. Examining the room gave her a moment to catch her breath. The round tables were covered with elegant white cloths and circled a makeshift dance floor. The lighting was muted but the balloons and the dance music — courtesy of a disc jockey — made the occasion more festive. At the lead table, Foster assisted Kayla to her seat. Tyler and Xavier did the same for Iris and Lily. Donovan held her chair. Chivalry was alive.

"Thank you." Rose took her chair, forcing her attention from Donovan's mesmerizing gaze.

Conversation topics were light during the salad course: the weather, the workweek, interesting plans for the weekend. Servers brought their entrées, an unexpectedly delicious dinner of spicy chicken, smashed potatoes and asparagus.

Rose realized that as the two families — the Andersons and Beharies — grew more comfortable with each other, the conversation became more animated. Laughter flowed around the table. She enjoyed the banter between Foster, Kayla, Xavier, Tyler and Donovan. It reflected the wealth of love and trust they shared, and their unbreakable bond. Their closeness was similar to the relationship she had with her sisters.

Dessert was a sinfully rich, double-layered fudge walnut brownie. Rose sliced a portion of the pastry. The tastes of the confectioner's sugar, fudge and cocoa burst on her tongue and radiated within her mouth.

"You look as though you've just accepted an indecent proposal." Donovan's low voice was rich with humor.

Rose felt a blush rising into her cheeks. She sneaked a quick peek at him, seated on her right. "I was just . . . enjoying the pastry."

"Aren't you going to try your dessert, dear?" Kayla questioned Lily, who sat between Donovan and Xavier.

"No, thank you. I'm full." Lily's expression belied her denial. "Dinner was wonderful."

"Ah, but it wouldn't be complete without dessert." Kayla smiled encouragingly.

"I couldn't." Lily shook her head. Her expression was full of regret.

Rose looked away in rising irritation. Lily was on another one of her diets. Why did her sister insist on starving herself when she had a figure women would kill for?

"Do you want to share mine?" Xavier's voice was low.

Still, Rose heard his invitation to Lily. She looked toward them with surprise.

"Yes, thank you." Lily grinned.

Xavier didn't return Lily's smile. Instead, with somber intensity, he cut the brownie in half. He put one half on his napkin and offered the plate with the other half to Lily.

Between bites of brownie, Rose exchanged an Isn't-This-Interesting look with Iris, who was seated on her left. Unfortunately, Lily seemed clueless to the fact that Xavier was flirting with her.

"That's my cue." Foster clamped his large hand on Tyler's broad shoulder as he stood from the table. "Wish me luck."

"Good luck, but you don't need it." Tyler watched his father cross the floor, then mount the stairs to the stage in front of the ballroom.

Rose leaned toward to Donovan. "What did I miss? What was his cue?"

Donovan shifted closer to her. "Finishing his dessert was Foster's cue to take the stage and address our associates."

Rose wasn't sure what Donovan had just said. It had something to do with Foster and dessert. Donovan's nearness had muddled his message. His scent — sandalwood and musk — distracted her. Or maybe it was his strong, striking features that made it hard for her to decipher the words coming out of his firm, well-shaped lips. Either way, Foster had begun his speech before Rose could focus.

"Thank you for coming." Foster looked confident and comfortable behind the microphone. "We're here tonight to celebrate Anderson Adventures' historic launch of our latest gaming product, Osiris' Journey." He laughed as the room erupted into shouts and cheers. Associates rose to give each other a standing ovation for their accomplishment.

Rose stood along with everyone else at the lead executive table. Swept up by the excitement of the people around her, she shouted and applauded with everyone else.

Still smiling, Foster raised his arms to reclaim their attention. "Osiris' Journey is undeniably our most successful game launch in company history. That's really saying something, because we've had some impressive launches."

Foster paused again as the company's associates acknowledged their past successes with raucous cheering. "Tonight, I want to celebrate my son, Tyler, our vice president of product development." Foot stamping joined the cheers this time. "As well as Iris Beharie, our marketing consultant." The shouts and applause that followed Foster's announcement filled Rose's heart with pride. "And all of you for your excellent work. We never take you for granted. Thank you." Foster took a moment to applaud his associates. "Now let's dance!"

Foster grinned as he left the stage. The disc jockey turned up the volume on her sound system. The makeshift dance floor filled quickly. Rose was impressed by the event Anderson Adventures had arranged for their associates. A movement from the corner of her eye caught her attention. She turned to find Xavier leading Lily onto the dance floor. Her eyes widened.

She stilled at the look of pleasure that swept across Kayla's face. Xavier's mother must be hopeful that her son was recovering from his disappointing relationship. Kayla's expression shifted to affection as she accepted Foster's invitation to dance. Beside Rose, Iris and Tyler excused themselves to find a spot on the rapidly filling floor.

She and Donovan were the only ones left at the table. Rose stiffened. She was afraid to look at him. If she did, would he ask her to dance? Did she want to dance — with him? The music was so inviting. What could one dance hurt? Still, maybe it would be better if they just sat here and talked.

"Have you made up your mind?" Donovan's voice was so close. She thought she'd felt his breath against her skin where the scooped back of her black dress bared her shoulders.

"What do you mean?" Rose convinced herself to face him. He was so close she could see the brown flecks in his hazel eyes.

"Right now, you're asking yourself whether you should dance with me." A ghost of a smile curved his sexy lips. "Consider this — your reunion is two months away. And we'll have to convince people that we're lovers."

Rose's breath caught in her throat. That word on his lips should be illegal. "I know."

"I'm sure we would've danced at least a few times in our relationship." Donovan stood and removed his pewter-gray jacket. His muscled shoulders flexed beneath his pale rose shirt. "Come on."

Donovan cupped her elbow to help her to her feet. His hand slid down her arm in a long, lingering caress. He caught her palm and clasped it to his. Rose's skin heated beneath his touch. Donovan drew her onto the crowded dance floor. Rose gave his back a narrow-eyed stare. Had he done that on purpose?

He guided Rose past shaking, shimmying bodies along the way, he exchanged warm greetings with associates. It was obvious they not only respected the sales executive, they admired him. When Donovan had arrived almost at the center of the floor, he turned to Rose. Then the music changed.

She stilled. How could the DJ go from a bass-driven dance song to a slow-moving ballad? Who did that? Rose groaned. Was it with disappointment — or desire?

Donovan's eyes twinkled as though he was once again reading her mind. *How many women have swooned under that look?*

He looped his arms loosely around her waist and lowered his head to whisper in her ear. "Come here, lover."

"Stop calling me that." Rose scowled up at him. She ignored the way his words heated her blood. Though his smile invited her to share the joke, she wasn't amused. She braced her hands lightly on his shoulders, then tried her best to ignore him. It wasn't easy. His cologne surrounded her. The scent was almost as intoxicating as the expression in his eyes. If he did a commercial for the fragrance, the company would move a lot of product.

"A penny for your thoughts." He lowered his head to whisper in her ear again. This time, he must have felt her shiver in response. His arms tightened around her. Rose swallowed a moan.

"My mind is a perfect blank." *Wishful thinking.* Her thoughts tumbled over themselves, each one focused on him: his shoulder muscles flexing, then relaxing beneath her palms; his scent teasing her senses; his body brushing against hers; his warmth seeping into her skin.

"Do you want to know what I'm thinking?" He didn't whisper in her ear this time, thank goodness.

"Not especially." Rose kept her attention on their surroundings. Tyler and Iris danced cheek to cheek. Nearby, Xavier and Lily barely moved as they chatted like long-lost friends reunited. In the distance, Foster and Kayla beamed at each other.

"It was your idea that we pretend to be madly in love." Donovan continued to exhibit a twisted sense of humor.

The man was impossible. Rose's gaze chastised him. "I never said anything about being madly in love."

"Are you still in love with Ben?"

Rose stiffened. "Definitely not."

The bold, dark slashes of Donovan's eyebrows lifted. "Methinks the lady doth protest too much."

"I'm serious." Rose's gaze drifted around the room again.

"You're not going to be able to convince him of that if you can't even dance with me."

"I *am* dancing with you."

Donovan chuckled. Her thighs quivered as though he'd touched them. "Rose, a door would feel more at ease. You need to relax."

"I *am* relaxed." Another lie. She was getting good at this.

Donovan Carroll was too handsome, too sexy, too charming. Just like Benjamin. It wasn't easy letting down her guard with another player. She'd spent the past seventeen months developing her Anti-Player Defense Shield. Donovan's expression grew serious. "If we're going to pull off this fake relationship, you're going to have to trust me."

Mercifully, the music stopped. Rose led Donovan back to the executive table. *Why does it feel as though I'm running away from him?*

Maybe he was right. She needed to make a greater effort to relax around him. But she was caught between a rock and a hard place. To save face in front of her cheating ex-fiancé, she'd have to pretend to be in love with another player.

What made me think this would be a good idea?

"This is a photo of Van and me at one of his company's functions." Rose loaded onto her cellular phone the picture of her and Donovan that Iris had taken during the launch celebration last Friday. She passed the phone to Maxine Ellerson, who was seated beside her at the booth in the restaurant.

"He's very handsome." Maxine gave Rose an appreciative smile. Her ebony eyes twinkled with mischief. "Much more handsome than Ben." She handed the phone to Claudia, who sat across the table from her.

It was the third Friday of July. The former law school classmates had gotten together at their regular restaurant for their monthly dinner. They'd finished their meals and paid their bills. Now they were enjoying a final drink before saying goodbye. The restaurant was still packed. The murmur of conversations from other tables flowed around them. The scents of exotic spices and savory stews filled the air.

Rose had asked Iris to take the photo of

her with Donovan so that she could show it to her Constant Classmates. She hoped the other women would accept the photo as proof that her "boyfriend" was real.

"Ooh, he *is* handsome." Claudia Brentwood-Washington pressed a well-manicured hand to the scooped neckline of her cream blouse. "He could be a model."

"So this is your mystery boyfriend." Tasha Smalls took the phone from Claudia and stared at the image on the device's display screen. Despite her sour tone, Tasha's expression held grudging admiration. "He's attractive, if you like that type."

"Give us a break, Tasha." Maxine sipped her ice water. The deep gold of her linen dress complemented her cocoa skin. "You know you like his type."

"What type is that?" Rose felt defensive.

"Handsome." Maxine wiggled her arched brows. Her close-cropped natural emphasized her large, dark eyes.

"He could be an underwear model." Claudia's boney chestnut features glowed with interest.

Rose frowned at the married mother of one. *Don't drool on my cell.* "I'll take that back." She reclaimed the phone from Tasha.

Tasha gave her a startled look and gestured toward the phone. "What's his name again?"

"Van Carroll." Rose tossed Tasha a look. She hadn't given her classmates a name last month. She hadn't had one to share. Tasha still wasn't buying her boyfriend story. Was the other woman going to pose a problem?

Claudia extended her hand, palm up. "Can I take another look?"

Rose returned her phone to her purse. "No, you cannot."

Claudia lowered her hand. Her disappointment was palpable.

"What did you say Van does for a living?" Tasha's question reclaimed Rose's attention. Suspicion was stamped all over the other woman's round, brown face.

"I hadn't told you what he did, but I'll tell you now. He's the vice president of sales for Anderson Adventures."

Maxine stared at her. "The computer gaming company?"

Rose turned to the woman seated beside her. "That's right. They're very successful with computer games."

"I know." Maxine was almost shaking with excitement. "I own several of their games. I preordered their newest release, Osiris' Journey, last month. I can't wait."

Tasha leaned back on the booth seating,

crossing her arms over her navy blouse. "You're a grown, educated woman. Why are you playing little-boy computer games?"

Maxine shrugged. "They're fun and interesting. And Anderson Adventures' games also are educational."

Tasha shook her head, tossing her thin braids around her shoulders. "That's probably the reason you're not married."

Rose scowled. "There's no need for that, Tasha."

"Don't worry about it, Rose." Maxine squeezed Rose's forearm where it lay on the table. "I don't take Tasha seriously."

Tasha gasped. "Why not?"

"Tasha, I love you, but you're jealous of everyone." Maxine's kind smile softened the chastisement. "Look at the way you're interrogating Rose. She doesn't have to tell us every personal detail of her life. She's not a public figure. She's entitled to her privacy."

Tasha leaned into the table, splitting her attention between Rose and Maxine. "You have a man who's successful and makes Ben Shippley look like SpongeBob. You should be bragging about him. Instead you're keeping your relationship a secret. Why?"

"After Ben, you can understand my need to be cautious with my relationships, can't you?" Rose wasn't lying. She wasn't answering the question, either.

"I understand." Claudia nodded her agreement. "You were with Ben for more than two years. Then you found out he wasn't the man he'd pretended to be."

It hurt to have her failed relationship summed up so succinctly. But it was the truth. Benjamin had practically left her at the altar. She'd felt like a fool. Sometimes she still did.

Rose shifted her attention from her friends to the dark wood and jewel tones of the restaurant's interior. But instead of the tables and booths arranged across the wood flooring, she saw images of her past, scenes that should have alerted her to Benjamin's lies: late nights, missed appointments, abrupt phone calls. How could she have trusted him so blindly? How could she not have known he'd been cheating on her for years? She would never allow anyone to make her feel like a fool again.

"Will we meet him at the reunion?" Maxine's voice still bounced with enthusiasm.

Rose snapped back from the past. "Yes, he's coming with me."

"Oh, great." Maxine's joyous tone made Rose smile. "I'm excited to meet someone who works for my favorite computer gaming company."

"I can't wait to see him in the flesh." Claudia's reaction drew Rose's suspicion.

"Neither can I." Tasha gave Rose a challenging look.

Rose returned Tasha's gaze with equanimity, but inside she was unsure. How much more of a fool would she feel if people discovered her relationship with Donovan wasn't real?

CHAPTER 6

Benjamin Shippley's name didn't appear on Rose's ringing cell phone. That's because she'd taken him out of her directory. But Rose still recognized her ex-fiancé's personal phone number.

Temper raised its ugly head. She stabbed her cellular phone screen to accept the call, but then she stopped herself before she spoke. Rose closed her eyes and gritted her teeth. Benjamin couldn't know he could still get a reaction from her. She drew a deep breath and channeled her inner Lily.

"I told you to lose my number." Rose was pleased with her cool, measured delivery.

"Is that the way you're going to greet me?" Benjamin had the nerve to sound surprised by her tone. The snake. "It's been almost two years, Rose."

"And there still isn't any reason for you to contact me." A pulse pounded in Rose's temple. Why was she allowing Benjamin to get to her? He didn't mean anything to her anymore.

"Can't we at least try to keep our relationship professional?" He sounded so reasonable even as he made his unreasonable request.

"We don't have a relationship. And I'd prefer to keep it that way." Rose stood from her mocha-brown sofa, setting aside the romantic suspense novel she'd been reading, and paced her family room.

"We're adults, aren't we?" Benjamin's voice was smooth and unruffled.

Rose wanted to jump through the phone and tear him apart. His call had caught her off guard. The snake obviously had prepared himself for this conversation. How long had he been planning to ambush her? Rose pictured her ex-fiancé. In her mind, he was wearing a dark, tight T-shirt to show off his biceps and flat stomach. His shorts would be a size too small, drawing attention to his glutes and long legs.

"I've always been a responsible adult. The same can't be said of you." She clenched her fist and closed her eyes. That was more like angry Rose than reasonable Lily. She'd have to watch that.

Her footsteps carried her into her kitchen where she'd had a solitary lunch not long before. Had Benjamin and his new wife already eaten? Resentment burned her. Benjamin had given another woman the husband and family he'd promised her. He was about to become a father while Rose had become a hermit.

"I can tell you're still upset over what happened." Benjamin's words shocked her out of her musings.

Had he lost his mind? Rose opened her mouth to scald him with her famous temper. Once again at the last minute, reason intruded. How would Lily respond to Benjamin? "No one likes being lied to. And you lied to me for two years."

"I've already apologized. Do you expect me to do it again?" Benjamin was showing cracks in his calm. Rose smiled to herself.

"No, but I do expect you never to call me again. Goodbye." Rose started to hang up, but Benjamin's frantic shouts made her hesitate.

"Rose, wait. Wait. I need to speak with you."

"What is it?" Not that she was interested in what he had to say.

"I called you to discuss the panel." The agitation was clear in Benjamin's voice. He paused, but when Rose didn't speak, he continued. "We're going to be presenting on the same panel."

"I know." That was the extent of Rose's interest in this discussion. "I'll see you then."

"Rose, wait. I think we should get together to discuss the topic and how best to present it."

Oh, heck, no. "I'm not meeting with you to discuss anything. Ever."

"There are three of us on the panel. It's not as though we're going to be meeting privately."

"You can email your thoughts to me and the other presenter, if this is something you want to discuss." If his email appeared in her inbox, she'd mark it as spam. Rose pivoted on her heels and strode back into her family room.

"We should meet, Rose." Benjamin's voice was adamant. "It's better to discuss these things in person."

Rose hesitated beside her black leather sofa. "Why are you so nervous about this panel? We're discussing legislative updates and their impact on the judicial system. It's not that complicated."

"I want to be prepared." Benjamin's response seemed tense.

"You're a lawyer. Do your research, and you'll be prepared."

"Research has always come so easily to you."

Rose frowned. *What was he saying?* "It's part of my job."

"I'm asking for your help in preparing for this panel so that I don't make a fool of myself."

Rose shook her head. He was amazing. "What makes you think I'd help you?"

"It's been almost two years, Rose. Why are you still holding a grudge?"

"If you didn't think you could research the discussion topic, why did you accept the invitation to participate on the panel?"

"Because I saw that you were on the panel, and I wanted the chance to spend time with you again."

Rose caught her breath. Her mind spun with the implications of his words. Then she burst into laughter. She leaned her head back, allowing the waves of hilarity to rise up from her stomach, expand her chest, then roll from her throat.

"*What* is so funny?" Benjamin sounded as though he was clenching his teeth.

"You must think I'm such a fool." Rose wiped the tears from her eyes. "There you sit with your pregnant wife — yes, I've heard that she's pregnant — expecting me to believe that you'd jump at the opportunity to spend time with me again. Why would *I* want to spend time with *you*? What makes you think I'm not with someone?"

"Are you?"

"Goodbye, Ben. Don't call me again." Rose ended the call even though Benjamin was still speaking. Let the snake stew on that until the reunion.

Rose tossed her phone onto her sofa and watched it bounce on the seat cushion. She dragged her fingers through her hair, wanting to pull on it. He must think she's an idiot to try that come-on with her.

"I wanted the chance to spend time with you again." Rose mocked him to the empty room. "Urgh!"

She spun on her bare heels and marched across the family room. This was yet another example of why she needed a fake boyfriend, and why the farce had to work. She couldn't bear it if people realized she'd been celibate since her failed engagement.

Rose strode back to her sofa. She snatched her phone from the cushion and dialed Donovan's number.

Donovan answered on the second ring. "Hello?"

"It's Rose. We need to talk."

"All right." His acquiescence eased her temper.

"May I stop by?"

"Sure." He gave her his address and directions to find him.

"Thanks. I'm on my way."

Donovan watched Rose assess his living room. He'd decorated it in deep greens and warm blues, with comfortable furniture against stark white walls. The furnishings were meant to make his guests feel welcomed and relaxed. She seemed neither.

"What's happened?" He followed her into the room. The polished hardwood flooring felt cool against his bare feet.

She turned to him. Her glossy, black hair swung above her narrow shoulders. Her long slender body was clothed in black capris and a gray tunic. "What do you mean?"

"You wouldn't be here if something hadn't happened." He stopped an arm's length from her.

"Am I that transparent?" Rose rested her purse on his mahogany coffee table and paced away from him.

"Yes." Donovan smiled to soften his stark response.

Rose lowered her head. "Ben called."

Donovan felt curiously irritated by that announcement. He studied Rose's back, forcing his gaze to remain above her well-rounded posterior. "Does he do that a lot?"

"I haven't heard from him in almost two years." She spoke with her back to him. "Actually, it's been one year, five months and two days."

"Not that you've been counting." Donovan shoved his hands into the front pockets of his gray cargo shorts. "Why did he call?"

"He wanted to discuss our panel presentation." Rose finally faced him. "I told him to do his own research. There isn't any reason for us to get together."

"Do you think he was making an excuse to see you again?" His irritation was rising. Did Benjamin still have feelings for Rose? *Why does that thought bother me?*

"No, I don't." Rose rubbed her forehead. "He said he was afraid of making a fool of himself during the panel. I believe him." There was vicious satisfaction in Rose's words.

"I have a feeling there's a lot more to your background with your ex than a simple breakup." Donovan propped his shoulder against the wall beside his entertainment center. "Care to clue me in?"

"Of course there's more to our breakup. Isn't there always?"

"Not necessarily. Sometimes people just

drift apart." Donovan braced himself to hear about Benjamin Shippley.

Did he break your heart? And is it still broken after one year, five months and two days?

Rose sighed. She wandered to the other side of the room, near his overstuffed couch. "Ben cheated on me. Luckily, I found out before the wedding."

Donovan hadn't expected that. What kind of fool would cheat on a woman like Rose? "I'm sorry."

"So am I." Rose ran her hand over the arm of his sofa. The gesture was like a caress. "I'm sorry I ever dated him, sorry I agreed to marry him. Sorry I ever met him."

"How did you two meet?"

"We'd been friends in law school, but we lost touch after graduation."

"Then you weren't close friends." He couldn't resist pointing that out.

"Do you want to hear this or not?"

"Please continue."

Rose slowly circled his living room. "We bumped into each other a few years after law school. One thing led to another, then two years later, he proposed. It wasn't until six months into planning our wedding that I realized he'd been cheating on me."

"I'm sorry. That must have hurt."

"More than I could've imagined." Rose stilled. "In the two and a half years we'd been together, he'd slept with ten different women."

"What?" He couldn't have heard her correctly. But the pain etched into her profile told him he had.

"He'd been cheating on me since we'd started dating." Rose wrapped her arms around herself. "He'd go out with other women, sleep with them, then come home to me. I thought he was working. Then I realized even I wasn't working such long hours with so many overnight trips."

"So you confronted him?"

She nodded. "And I canceled the wedding. I later learned from a mutual friend that he'd married his last girlfriend on the same date, in the same church, with the same reception hall and caterer that I'd booked."

"Wow." Donovan shook his head in disbelief. "The guy has a lot of nerve."

"His wife's pregnant. They're living the happily-ever-after he'd promised me."

"Don't believe that. Not for a minute." Donovan straightened from the wall, pulling his hands from his shorts pockets. "People like Ben don't change overnight. If he cheated on you, he's cheating on her."

"Maybe he's changed now that he's about to become a father."

Why was she torturing herself with these questions? Did she want them to be true? "The fact that he tried a line on you shows that he's still a serial cheater."

Rose exhaled. She massaged her right shoulder. "You're right."

Donovan saw the strain on her elegant, honey features. He crossed to her, then cupped her left cheek with his hand. Her skin was soft and warm beneath his palm.

"I'm sorry Ben lied to you and treated you so poorly. But remember, Rose, Ben's behavior reflects only on him, not on you." Donovan couldn't resist the urge to smooth his thumb over her silky cheek. "You're an intelligent, beautiful, sexy woman. You deserve better."

Rose searched his eyes. She cupped his hand and lowered it from her face. "Did you hear that on the *Dr. Phil* show?"

"Do you watch it?"

She gave him the smile he'd been hoping for, then released his hand. "We should probably get the details of our fake relationship straight." Rose settled onto one corner of his sofa. "I showed our picture to some friends last night. They had a lot of questions."

Donovan sat on the other end of the couch. His palm burned where he'd touched her cheek. He fisted his hand to keep from touching her again. "What did you tell them?"

"The truth — your name, where you work and what you do." She tossed him a smile that was strained around the edges. "One of my friends is a big fan of Anderson Adventures' computer games."

"Only one? Hopefully, by the end of our deal, they'll all have our games."

"Before you turn my reunion into a marketing venue for your products, let's focus on our original plan, shall we?" Rose arched an eyebrow. "We should keep our story as close to the truth as possible. The truth is easier to remember. Iris and Ty introduced us."

"Good idea. But we should probably tell people we've known each other for longer than a month."

"You have a point." Rose inclined her head. "If people knew we met in June, they'd think we got together just for the reunion."

"Imagine that."

"You know what I mean." She gave him a dry look. "We can't be too obvious."

"We could tell people we met in March.

That's when Ty met Iris."

"Perfect." Rose nodded decisively, then stood from the sofa. "I'm glad we could agree on those details."

"So am I." *What was happening here?*

"Thanks for letting me interrupt you. Enjoy the rest of your afternoon." Rose turned to lead him toward his front door.

"Aren't there other things that we need to discuss?"

Rose paused in his doorway and faced him. "Like what?"

She seriously didn't know. They needed to discuss what they were like as a couple. What they did, what they enjoyed, what set them off; everything that made a couple a couple. Romance. But maybe that discussion should wait. Rose needed time and space after Benjamin's phone call.

"We'll work everything out." He stepped aside to let her leave. "We have time."

Her brown gaze was curious. "Yes, we do."

Donovan watched her leave. They now had the framework of their story straight, but they'd need more than words to convince her friends. His pulse picked up. Donovan was beginning to look forward to preparing for Rose's reunion.

On Monday morning, Donovan realized he

was about to get an earful from Cecil Lowell. He recognized the younger man's number on his cellular phone display. Somehow the most junior member of the shelter's board of directors had convinced himself that he had a lot to teach the veterans. But right now, Donovan's greatest concern was that Cecil continued to ignore his request not to contact him at work.

"What can I do for you, Cecil?" Donovan worked hard to keep his impatience from his voice.

"We need to call another special meeting of the subcommittee." The urgency in Cecil's voice demanded Donovan's full attention.

"What's happened?" Donovan remembered to lock his computer system before turning away from his monitor.

"We need to strategize what we're going to do if the city council rejects our statement." The observation was strange coming from Cecil, who hadn't supported the board's statement in the first place.

Donovan sat back on his black, padded executive chair. He struggled again to keep his impatience from his tone. "What makes you think the council will reject our statement?"

"As I made clear after my review of the

statement, I have reservations about your girlfriend's work."

Donovan started to deny the personal relationship between him and Rose until he remembered that they were indeed trying to project that image. They'd agreed to maintain their pretense within both of their social circles to help keep their story straight. It also would protect them against having their cover blown by mutual acquaintances they may not be aware of. Six degrees of separation, you never knew who you may know.

He pinched the bridge of his nose. "Cecil, any reservations you have come from your opposition to the statement in general."

"No, they stemmed from the fact that the arguments against the pawnshop weren't well formulated."

Donovan swallowed his laughter. "Where did you get your law degree, Cecil?"

"I don't need a law degree to recognize the arguments in the statement are weak." Cecil's tone was dismissive. "I realize you're impressed with your girlfriend's work, but as I made clear during our review, I'm not."

Donovan sat up, fisting his left hand on his modular Plexiglas desk. "Rose is more than my girlfriend. She's an experienced lawyer and an associate with a prestigious law firm."

Cecil sighed. "I know we needed a lawyer who'd represent us pro bono, but your decision to work with your girlfriend doesn't show good judgment. I think you should know that I'm going to challenge your presidency for the board of directors."

Donovan hadn't expected this. "You're going to ask the board for a special election to choose a new president in the middle of the term?"

"That's right. We need a chairman with better vision for the shelter. We can't continue down this road. It's too destructive."

Donovan was intrigued. "And you're going to suggest the board elect *you* as its next president?"

"I realize I'm the junior member, but it's time for new blood and fresh ideas. You've been wrong on too many things."

The accusation stung. Donovan took a calming breath, drawing in the scent of fresh coffee. "Such as?"

"The pawnshop." Cecil raised his voice. "I gave you a list of reasons why the board should support the shop moving into the neighborhood."

His list had included a series of unsupported predictions. It had given Donovan grave concerns about Cecil's critical thinking skills. He rubbed the back of his neck.

117

Donovan pictured Cecil making this call from his office desk at the bank. Did the young executive not have enough work to occupy his time?

"The majority of members voted to oppose the shop." Donovan hadn't forgotten that Cecil was the only member who thought the shop would have a positive impact on the struggling community.

"If I were chair, I wouldn't have allowed the vote." Cecil snorted. "I'd have convinced the members that the pawnshop would benefit the shelter."

"You tried that. No one supported you." Donovan's memory flashed back to Cecil going on for ten minutes, reading his memo on what he predicted would be the benefits of having the pawnshop in the community. Kim Lee had finally cut him off.

"As a new business in the community, it would be in the pawnshop owner's interest to support the shelter. It also would bring new customers into the neighborhood who would then see the services we offer to the homeless."

Donovan didn't have time to humor Cecil. He needed to return to work. "I'm glad you're willing to make a greater commitment to the shelter. But we don't need a special meeting to strategize a response to the city council's decision. We can wait until we hear from them."

"I disagree." Cecil's tone was adamant.

Donovan wasn't impressed. "I'm still in charge. We can discuss proposed responses to the council's decision during our regular meeting."

"That's two weeks away. Suppose the council makes its decision before then?" Cecil sounded agitated.

"Then we'll meet sooner." Donovan turned back to his monitor. "I'm sorry, Cecil, but I need to get back to work."

"Oh, I'm sorry. Did my concern for the homeless take you away from your computer games?" Cecil's sarcasm wasn't lost on Donovan.

But instead of irritating him, Donovan chose to be amused.

"As always, Cecil, your concern is appreciated. I'll let you get back to work now." He recradled his phone and returned to the sales plan he was drafting for one of the games in development.

Donovan didn't want to stifle Cecil's enthusiasm. He was right that the board of directors could use fresh, young voices. Donovan was the second-youngest person on the board. Most of the members were in their late fifties and early sixties. Cecil could prove to be a strong asset for the board for years to come. But the young executive needed guidance to better focus his passion and creativity.

He also needed to learn patience. Donovan wasn't ready to give up his position as board president. And he wouldn't allow Cecil to malign Rose to get his way.

CHAPTER 7

"Ms. Beharie, Donovan Carroll is here to see you." Mai Liu made the announcement to Rose over the phone minutes before noon on Tuesday. The Apple & Spencer LLC's receptionist sounded mildly curious, which was understandable. Rose never received personal visits at the law firm's offices.

"Thanks, Mai. I'll be right there." Rose recradled her telephone receiver.

What was Donovan thinking to show up at her place of business unannounced? She stood from her desk and shrugged into her sapphire blazer. She had to establish a few ground rules with him. Rose crossed the thick, beige carpet and walked out of her door.

The heels of her dark blue pumps tapped against the marble tile as she strode past the rows of tan cubicles. The work areas for administrative and support staff were surrounded by the dark wood doors and glass walls of the firm's partners and associates. Some of the staff had already left for lunch, including Rose's administrative assistant. Others appeared to be working while they ate. Rose descended the wide, winding metal-and-tile staircase that led to Apple & Spencer's reception area. She paused at the base of the stairs.

Donovan stood with his back to her as he examined the abstract painting mounted to the opposite wall. Rose took the opportunity to study the man just as carefully. His appearance was deceptively casual in a caramel jersey and warm brown slacks. But the fine material of his clothing marked him as a man of means. The strength and power beneath the well-cut cloth revealed him as someone not to be taken lightly. Donovan turned and smiled at her almost as though he had known she was there. Had he felt her staring? Rose's gaze dropped to the dozen long-stemmed red roses in his hand.

They walked toward each other, meeting in front of Mai's desk. Donovan leaned forward to kiss her cheek. In reflex, Rose started to pull back, and his lips grazed the corner of her mouth instead. His hazel eyes twinkled as he straightened.

"These are for you." He offered her the bouquet.

Rose took the gift and glanced toward Mai. The young woman was gazing at them as though she expected Donovan to sweep Rose off her feet and carry her onto the street.

"Thank you. They're beautiful." Beautiful and unexpected. Rose stepped back. "Why don't we go up to my office?"

She led the way upstairs, feeling awkward with Donovan's tall, silent presence beside her. In her three-inch heels, Rose matched the height of most of the men she knew and was taller than a few. But Donovan practically towered over her, making her feel almost petite. She would have laughed at that thought if she weren't so conscious of the attention directed their way.

She never received personal visits at the office. Since she'd left empty-handed and returned cradling a bouquet of red roses and baby's breath, she couldn't pass Donovan off as a client. She inclined her head at a couple of coworkers before she reached the sanctuary of her office. She stepped aside to allow Donovan to precede her, then pulled shut her thick maple door.

"Why are you here, Van?" Rose crossed the room and laid the roses on her desk.

"I'm getting into character." He stood in the center of her office, looking around.

123

"Wow, you are really tidy."

His comment distracted her from her follow-up question. Rose scanned her office, trying to imagine it from his perspective. Her wall-to-wall beige carpet and matching furniture gave her office a bright, spacious look. Her Plexiglas inbox was full but neat. Her laptop sat in the center of her ash-wood-and-Plexiglas modular desk. The blond wood bookcase behind her was crammed with case binders and reference books. In contrast to the whirlwind that was Donovan's office, she supposed her workspace seemed obsessively neat.

Rose propped a hip against the side of her desk. "What do you mean, you're getting into character?"

"I'm supposed to be your boyfriend." Donovan sat on one of the beige faux-leather guest chairs in front of her desk. "I'm doing the things a boyfriend should do."

Rose glanced down at her bouquet. She needed to get a vase for them. "Is that what your greeting was about?" She hadn't expected him to try to kiss her.

"Suppose we're at your reunion and one of your former classmates asks if I've ever been to your firm or whether I've ever bought you roses." Donovan settled back

124

on the chair and propped his right ankle onto his left knee.

Rose pulled her attention from his long, lean thigh and met his gaze. "We could just lie and say yes to both."

"We could." Donovan shrugged, the movement of his broad shoulders fluid under his dark jersey. "But we agreed to keep the story as close to the truth as possible. Our responses would be more authentic if we're working from memories rather than lies."

Rose's gaze dropped again to her bouquet. She hated to admit it, but the man had a point. Even though their whole relationship was make-believe, she couldn't imagine faking what she'd felt when she received these "just because" roses. "You're right."

Donovan's features brightened with his grin. "Something tells me I should mark this day with a ceremonial plaque."

"Don't push it." Rose gave him a dry look.

"With this one visit, we've already accomplished three things." Donovan stood. He was too close.

Rose straightened from her desk, putting space between them. "What are they?"

"I've seen where you work, met one of your coworkers." He closed the distance. "And I bought you roses."

Rose backed up. "That's a lot for people

who've only been in a relationship since March."

She glanced toward the glass walls of her office to see if anyone else had noticed that Donovan was crowding her. No one seemed to be paying attention to them, although she could be mistaken.

"It's just the beginning. Most importantly, we have to become more comfortable with each other. We have to learn to trust each other." Donovan closed the gap between them again. He was invading her personal space.

His scent, sandalwood and musk, enveloped Rose. His body heat spread into her clothing. Rose forced herself to hold her ground and his gaze. "I'm comfortable with you," she lied.

Donovan chuckled. It was a low, rumbling sound that she felt vibrate in her lower abdomen. "Then why do you flinch every time I touch you?"

"I don't."

Donovan leaned in — Rose reared back. His sexy lips curved in a smug smile. "Yes, you do." He straightened. "You can't do that at your reunion. You'll give us away."

"I'll have that under control before the reunion."

"How?"

The man was frustrating, especially when he was right. "Fine, we'll spend time together. But we can't go from zero to sixty. Back up. If you get any closer, you'll be in my suit."

Donovan took a step back, and Rose breathed more easily.

"Sorry." He flashed her a friendly smile.

Rose ignored it and the way it weakened her knees. "That's fine. What do you propose we do to get more comfortable with each other?"

Donovan cocked his head. "Why don't we start with something simple, like lunch?"

Rose checked her silver Timex wristwatch. "I can do that."

This was a surprise. In a matter of minutes, they'd agreed on two things: roses and lunch. She'd begun to think they'd never come to a consensus on anything. Their constant disagreements wouldn't play well during her reunion. They needed to project a loving and harmonious relationship. Benjamin — and his pregnant wife — had to believe she'd found her happily-ever-after with the man of her dreams.

Rose collected her purse from the bottom drawer of one of her file cabinets. She swallowed a sigh. Would she ever find her happy ending? Was she even meant to have one?

She slid a sideways look at Donovan as she adjusted the strap of her purse onto her shoulder. So far, all she'd come up with was an agreement with a stranger for a fake relationship. It didn't seem that her fairy-tale ending was destined to happen anytime soon.

"After you." Donovan stepped aside, then winked at her.

Rose's heart fluttered at the casual gesture. At least her make-believe prince was undeniably handsome and incredibly sexy. As far as fake relationships went, this one had its perks. Too bad it was all a farce.

Donovan took in the happy expressions of the people gathered around Lily Beharie's dining table on Wednesday night. He could still smell the spicy grilled chicken, warm, buttery mashed potatoes and tangy salad dressing. For dessert, the ladies had served hot apple pie à la mode.

It was more than a week after Donovan had paid the surprise visit to Rose's law firm with the dozen red roses and suggested they get to know each other better before her reunion. Tonight was another step in that direction — they were now getting to know each other's friends and family.

Lily was seated at the head of the table,

with Xavier to her left and Tyler on her right. Xavier seemed to be paying particular attention to Lily. Although Lily was friendly, she didn't seem encouraging. Rose sat at the other end of the table on Donovan's left. Iris sat across from him beside Tyler. They were all dressed in business clothes since they'd met right after work.

Donovan had persuaded Rose to extend a dinner invitation to him, Tyler and Xavier during their spontaneous lunch last Tuesday. He'd used the excuse that they needed to "better develop" their fake relationship. Rose had seemed dubious at first, almost as though she'd known Donovan just wanted to spend more time with her but apparently his fake girlfriend believed there was safety in numbers.

Lily caught Donovan's gaze as she returned her glass of ice water to the table. "Have you received a response to your statement from the city?"

"We haven't heard anything yet." Donovan turned his attention to Rose. "I don't know what's taking so long."

"It's only been two weeks." Rose's voice was patient as she reminded him. "However, if I don't hear anything from the council by Friday, I'll contact them for an update on Monday."

"Fair enough. Thanks." Donovan gazed around the table. He was encouraged by how well the evening was going. "Why did you start the Beharie family dinners?"

"Our parents started it once we all moved back to Columbus after college and graduate school." Rose's voice was warm with happy memories.

"When Lily moved back into the house after they died, it seemed natural for us to continue the tradition." Iris cut into her pie and ice cream.

"It's a nice tradition." Donovan's observation was an understatement. He admired their tradition and the familial closeness it fostered. "I'm sorry for your loss."

"Thank you." Rose gave him a gentle smile. "Losing them was difficult."

"These dinners helped us deal with our grief." Lily toyed with her pie and ice cream.

Rose swallowed a bite of dessert. "The only difference is that we get together on Wednesdays instead of Sundays. We couldn't wait the whole week."

"No, we couldn't." Iris chuckled. "These have become great venting sessions to talk about heavy caseloads." She nodded toward Rose, then squeezed Tyler's forearm over the sleeve of his brown jersey. "And unreasonable clients."

"Hey, now." Tyler pretended to glower at her but the laughter in his eyes gave him away.

Xavier turned to Lily. "What do you vent about?"

Lily shrugged a shoulder beneath her pale pink blouse. "I don't have much to complain about."

"Lil is our therapist." Rose grinned. "She keeps Iris and me from going off the deep end."

"That's a full-time job." Lily sent her older sister a mocking look.

Donovan smiled. He was seeing a different side of Rose, a warm and loving side. She and her sisters shared an unbreakable bond of love, trust and commitment that went beyond sibling obligations.

Rose turned to Donovan. "So how did the three of you become friends? You're not from Columbus."

Donovan was surprised she'd asked a personal question. He swallowed his pie before answering. "No, I'm from Chicago. We met at college, New York University. Xavier and I became friends first. Then Ty enrolled and the three of us have been close ever since."

"Do you miss Chicago?" Rose's chocolate eyes remained focused on him.

Be careful what you wish for, Donovan reminded himself too late. Now that he'd caught Rose's interest, he was afraid of her learning too much about his past. "No, I don't have any ties to Chicago. I lost my parents a long time ago."

"I'm so sorry." A flash of pain crossed Rose's elegant features.

Xavier squeezed Donovan's shoulder. "Nothing can make up for losing parents, but at least he has family in Columbus now."

From across the table, Donovan saw the agreement on Tyler's face. It still amazed him how easily the Anderson family had accepted him despite his past — Xavier and Tyler as well as Foster and Kayla. He felt more like a blood relative than a close family friend and business associate.

Iris's chuckle eased the sudden emotion building in the room. "The first time I met the Anderson Adventures leadership team was during one of your meetings. It was more like a family gathering than an executive meeting."

"I'm sorry Foster and Kayla weren't able to join us tonight." Lily still played with her food.

"Perhaps they can join us if we do this again." Donovan tried to sound casual.

Rose's skeptical look told him he hadn't

quite managed it. "Will you gentlemen be doing the cooking?"

"I'm game. What about you guys?" Donovan looked from Tyler to Xavier.

"Sure." Xavier slid a glance toward Lily. The Beharie sister didn't seem to notice.

"All right, but maybe we should have it at my place." Tyler gave Donovan a pointed look. "At least we'd be confident of having clean dishes."

Good-natured laughter swept the table. Rose's soft, husky chuckles captivated Donovan. He could listen to her laughter for hours. And he could look at her for days, maybe forever? Her honey-toned features glowed; her warm, chocolate eyes sparkled. She was so different from the woman he'd met during lunch with Tyler and Iris. That woman put ice in his heart. This woman could steal it. The realization caused Donovan a frisson of unease.

Donovan settled onto his usual chair in front of Xavier's desk Thursday morning. Tyler was on the guest chair beside him. It was just before eight o'clock the morning after their dinner with the Beharie sisters.

"I'm glad you and Rose are able to help each other." Tyler cocked his head. "I'm sure that's lifted a weight from your shoulders."

"It has." That was one problem handled. But there were always others demanding attention.

Tyler sipped his coffee. "Does she know about your past?"

The question cast a shadow over the memory of last night's great food and even better company. "I haven't told her that I used to be homeless, if that's what you mean."

"Why not?" Xavier asked. "You don't have anything to be ashamed of."

"I know that." Donovan hadn't meant to sound defensive.

"You were a kid." Tyler shifted toward Donovan. "What happened to your family wasn't your parents' fault."

"The fact that my family wasn't to blame hasn't mattered to the women I've dated." Donovan stared into his oversize mug of coffee. He barely noticed the scent of dry-roasted coffee beans. "Once I tell them my family had been homeless at one point, they disappear."

Would Rose?

"Iris wouldn't react that way." Tyler's voice was adamant. "She's not judgmental. I don't think Rose and Lily are, either."

Xavier spread his hands. "And even if we're wrong, you and Rose are just pretending to be in a relationship. Why are you worried about her breaking up with you?"

Donovan shook off his irritation. Just because their relationship was fake didn't mean he couldn't enjoy it. "Rose wouldn't want her boyfriend — real or fake — to have a questionable past."

"Rose isn't a snob, and you don't have a questionable past." Tyler drank more coffee.

Donovan blew a breath. "You're basing your assumption about Rose on what you know about Iris. Just because Iris isn't a snob doesn't mean her sisters aren't."

"Lily's not a snob." Xavier's voice was flat.

"You don't even know her." Donovan held Xavier's gaze. "I know you're attracted to Lily. Rose is a very beautiful woman, too. But experience has taught me that outer beauty isn't an indication of what's inside."

"Experience has taught me the same." Xavier's tone was dry.

"I didn't mean to bring that up." Donovan exhaled, rubbing his forehead.

"Don't worry about it." Xavier cradled his coffee mug. "I may not have a great track record when it comes to reading other people, but I'm sure Ty and I are right."

"Besides, you're not homeless now." Tyler

shrugged a shoulder. "In fact, most people would consider you to be successful."

Xavier gestured toward Donovan with his free hand. "You're the vice president of sales for a multimillion-dollar company. Your past doesn't matter."

"Not to the two of you but it has to others." Donovan arched an eyebrow.

Xavier met his gaze. "You should tell her about your past. Don't risk having her hear about it from someone else."

Donovan frowned at the finance executive. "The only people who know that my father and I were once homeless are the two of you, Foster and Kayla."

"And two of your ex-girlfriends." Tyler's tone was dry.

Donovan drank more of his coffee. "I don't think Rose will run into my ex-girlfriends between now and September."

"Stranger things have happened." Xavier leaned back on his chair.

"This is the age of the internet." Tyler spread his hands. "It's not six degrees of separation anymore. Today, everything's just a click away."

Xavier nodded his agreement. "At least consider telling Rose."

Donovan looked from one friend to the other. Did they have a point? He wasn't looking forward to opening up about his past with Rose. Based on his experience, the discussion wouldn't end well. Was he wrong to want to enjoy their pretend romance for as long as possible? If only he knew how long his borrowed time would last.

CHAPTER 8

"So your boyfriend grew up homeless. How does that make you feel?" Tasha sipped her diet soda Friday evening. Her eyes searched Rose's expression as though mining for information.

Rose had accepted Tasha's invitation to dinner, just the two of them, when her friend had called that morning. She'd wondered what Tasha had wanted to discuss in private. Now she knew. It was fortunate that Rose's experience as a corporate lawyer had helped her develop a poker face. She held Tasha's inquisitive brown eyes without blinking.

"How did you hear about that?" Rose forced a casual voice to cover her unease. Her mind scrambled to anticipate Tasha's questions and her answers.

Tasha reared back on her seat at their table in the Ethiopian restaurant they frequented. Her eyes feigned concern.

"Didn't you know?"

Rose smiled. Her friend's attempts to get under her skin amused her. Tasha was so competitive and melodramatic. The other woman had laid the jacket of her mustard skirt suit on the empty chair beside her. The first two buttons of her ivory blouse were undone, giving a hint of cleavage.

Their conversation was interrupted when their server brought their separate dinner bills. The young man took their empty plates when he left.

"Of course I knew about Van's past. He told me." The lie rolled easily from Rose's lips. The muscles in her neck and shoulders tightened as she pinned her friend with a look. "Who told you?"

"I used to work with his ex-girlfriend, Whitley Maxwell." Tasha's eyes focused on Rose as though looking for a reaction. "Did he tell you about her?"

"I know Van has dated other women."

Tasha played with her braids. "Yes, well, she said she'd dated Van for almost a year before he told her that he and his family used to live on the streets. She was so disgusted by his deceit that she broke up with him."

"Isn't that a bit drastic? But her loss is my gain." Rose scanned her restaurant bill, then fished her credit card from her purse.

Her hand shook slightly with tension. She had to keep her responses vague, otherwise Tasha would realize she didn't have any idea what she was talking about. She took a calming breath, allowing the savory scents of the restaurant's food to distract her.

Rose stuck her credit card inside the bill folder and slid them beside Tasha's at the edge of the table.

How could Donovan's ex-girlfriend be so upset that he hadn't immediately told her about his past that she'd break up with him? Or was it that she was upset to learn that she'd been dating someone who'd once been so disadvantaged? Either way, she couldn't understand Whitley Maxwell's reaction.

Knowing his past, Rose was even more impressed by Donovan. That he'd been able to rise from such disadvantaged circumstances to become vice president of a multimillion-dollar company before the age of forty was a testament to his determination, efforts and intelligence. Was his background one of the reasons he was such a fierce champion for those who were homeless? Her heart warmed toward the silver-tongued salesman. He had much more substance than she'd at first suspected.

140

"Why didn't you tell us he'd been home-less?" Tasha's question pulled Rose out of her thoughts.

"There's no need for me to share every detail of Van's past with you, Claudia or Maxine." Rose held her former classmate's gaze. She wanted to make sure her position was clear. "The fact that he once was home-less is relevant in that it helped shape the person he is today. But it's not a mark against him. In fact, when I think of where he came from and where he worked to put himself, I can only admire him."

Tasha flipped back her hair. "Well, it does make you wonder who his friends are."

"I've met his friends. We should all have such warm, caring, decent people in our lives." Rose thought of Tyler, Xavier, Foster and Kayla. They were more like Donovan's family than his friends. Another testament to her fake boyfriend's character.

Why hadn't Donovan told her that he'd been homeless? Rose frowned at her half-empty glass of iced tea. Had he thought she'd react the same way his ex-girlfriend and Tasha had reacted? If so, she was of-fended — but she couldn't fault him. He could only base his decisions on his experi-ences, and his experiences apparently had been pretty bad.

Their server returned to take their payments. Rose watched the young man maneuver past the other dark wood tables arranged across the casual restaurant. Most of the other customers — groups of friends, some couples — appeared to have come to the locale straight from work just as she and Tasha had. The restaurant hummed with their murmured conversations, broken by occasional bursts of laughter.

"If you're so impressed with him, are you going to tell Claudia and Maxine about his past?" Tasha gave her a challenging look.

Was the other woman deliberately missing the point? "If he wants them to know, he'll tell them. It's not my place to." Rose lifted her glass of iced tea. The drink was cold against her sweaty palm.

Tasha pulled one of her braids forward to toy with it. "Are you going to tell Van that I spoke with his ex?"

"I don't keep secrets from Van. I'm sure you understand my need for complete honesty in my relationships." Rose gave Tasha a pointed look. She was certain the other woman got her reference to her failed relationship with Benjamin.

Donovan must not want her to know that he'd once been homeless. He'd had plenty of opportunity to bring up the matter while they'd worked on the statement for the city council or when they'd had lunch almost two weeks ago. The fact that he'd kept silent must mean he wanted to keep his history a secret. Rose would respect that. She wouldn't ask him about his past; she'd wait until he was comfortable enough to bring it up on his own.

The question was, would he ever be that comfortable with her?

"When you called, you said we had something very important to discuss." Rose closed her front door after letting Donovan into her house on Saturday afternoon.

"Thanks for letting me come over." Donovan walked past her to wait while she secured the door lock. Rose caught a whiff of musk and sandalwood. The scent was becoming familiar but hadn't lost any of its appeal.

"If it's about the statement, I'm going to follow up with the city on Monday." She led him into her living room, stopping in front of her black faux-leather love seat.

Rose stole a quick peek at Donovan as he surveyed her sparse living room. A garnet, short-sleeved T-shirt showcased his broad back and stretched over his well-defined biceps. His pale gray carpenter shorts were tailored to his lean hips. Her eyes lingered on his long legs. His muscles flexed and stretched as he explored her living room. His tight glutes made her fingers twitch. His profile — chiseled sienna features and clean-shaven head — could make a ton of money for a men's skin care company.

Donovan turned to her. "We need to talk about our relationship."

"What about it?" Rose's pulse picked up. Was he about to tell her that he'd been homeless at one point in his childhood?

Should I act casual or let him know Tasha already told me?

Donovan stepped forward, closing the distance between them. "I didn't know where you lived until today. If your class-mates knew I'd never been to your house, it would blow our cover."

Does this mean he isn't going to confide in me about his past? Why does that bother me?

"You're here now." Rose spread her arms to encompass her living room. "Would you like the nickel tour?"

She'd already vacuumed, cleaned her kitchen sink and put her laundry away. She'd even made her bed — but perhaps they'd skip that room. She glanced around her living room. How did it appear to Donovan? In comparison to the strong colors and welcoming furniture in his home, her black, white and pewter decor probably felt cold and sanitized.

"Not right now." He approached Rose, gesturing toward the love seat behind her. "May I?"

"Of course." Rose turned to move to the sofa.

Donovan caught her hand. "No, please join me. There's plenty of room." He used his hold on her hand to draw her down to the love seat beside him.

Rose blinked. He'd moved so quickly. She hadn't expected that. She lowered her gaze. Her hand looked almost dainty in his — small and slender, nearly swallowed by his much larger palm and fingers. Donovan's skin was so warm and a little rough to the touch. A sharp intake of breath drew his scent to her. She had the strongest urge to turn her hand and hold his, but she pulled away.

She settled into her corner of the love seat, increasing the distance between them. "Now that you know where I live, what more do we need to discuss?"

"As I've said, we should get to know each other better. We're not going to pull this off if we seem like strangers." Donovan's hazel eyes twinkled as though he knew she was this close to moving to the sofa.

"I thought we'd been doing that with your impromptu lunch last Tuesday and dinner with my sisters on Wednesday." Rose could still feel his skin against her palm. She fisted her hand on top of her black linen shorts.

Donovan's gaze dropped to her lap before returning to hers. The teasing lights in his eyes had been replaced with faint curiosity. "That was general research. Now we know about each other's bosses and coworkers, where we went to school, our childhood and our families. Surface stuff."

Rose frowned. "Actually, all I know about your family is that you're an only child and both of your parents are deceased." She hadn't realized until her dinner with Tasha that she didn't know anything about Donovan's childhood at all. He was very adept at deflecting questions about his past.

"That's really all there is to know." Donovan grew still as though assessing a potentially dangerous situation.

Is that what it was like when you were pulling a curtain over your past? Was every personal question a possible threat? Rose couldn't imagine living under that kind of strain.

"What did your parents do?"

"My father was an entrepreneur." Dono-

146

van gave her a crooked smile, full of disarming charm. "That's a fancy term for a one-man landscaping company. My mother was an administrative assistant with a shipping company."

"How did they die?" Rose's words were almost tentative.

"Cancer. Both of them." Donovan's response was brief and final. Rose read the message in his eyes: *Don't go there.*

"I'm sorry for your loss." Rose's response was more than words. She understood to an extent his pain. "My father died of cancer, too. My mother had a heart attack."

Losing both of her parents so quickly had been hard. She thanked God every day that she'd had her sisters to help her through the heartache. But Donovan had been alone. Who had he leaned on to help him through such devastating losses? He was a strong person, much stronger and more substantial than the carefree persona he projected had led her to believe.

"I'm sorry." A look of regret shifted across his handsome features.

"Thank you." Rose stood from the sofa. "I'm sorry. I should have offered you something to drink."

"I'm fine, thanks."

"All right." Rose started to sit back down.

Donovan captured her waist and redirected her to his lap. "I hadn't intended for our conversation to be so somber."

He smiled into her startled eyes. His jovial mask was back in place. Rose was glad he'd had that momentary lapse, though. She enjoyed the carefree charmer, but the brooding man of mystery also held an appeal.

Rose scowled down at him. "And by my sitting on your lap, what had you intended our *conversation* to be?"

"You have a very suspicious mind, Ms. Beharie." His smile grew into a grin. He wrapped his arms around her in a loose embrace as she tried to get up.

"And you have a very obvious technique. I can hear you just fine from my end of the love seat." Rose's hands tightened on Donovan's stone-like forearms, but she wasn't in a rush to leave his lap. She felt comfortable, as though she belonged here. It was odd.

"Don't you like to cuddle?"

"This isn't cuddling. It's kidnapping." Rose crossed her arms, straining to ignore the sensation of his muscled thighs beneath her bottom. It was a struggle not to squirm against him. "You're holding me against my will."

"You'd call an act of physical affection a felony?" Donovan chuckled low in his chest. Rose felt the vibrations against her arm.

"This doesn't feel like cuddling. You're too hard." Rose went still. Donovan's arched brow and the glint in his wicked hazel eyes sent heat rushing up her neck to her face. "You know what I mean."

"I don't think I do." His voice shook with laughter.

"Your body's too stiff." Rose could have sunk beneath the floor.

"Really?" Donovan cocked his head. "Is that what you meant to say?"

"Just let me go." Rose lowered her arms. She glared at him while her embarrassment burned hotter.

"I will. But first, tell me what turns you on in a man."

"Why would I tell you that?"

"It's something your boyfriend would know."

"You do realize that our relationship is fake."

"But we're trying to convince your friends that it's real." He held her gaze. "Just tell me what turns you on."

Was it her imagination or were her nipples getting hard? *Please don't let Van notice.* But her prayers were probably in vain; the sexy

149

salesman seemed to notice everything. Rose smothered a groan.

She wanted him to release her, but she was not going to play his self-indulgent games. "What turns you on? Oh, let me guess — petite, curvy women with long hair."

Donovan gave her a shrewd look. "Like your sister Lily? She's beautiful. But I don't have a type."

Of course not. He was an equal-opportunity player. "Then what's your turn-on?"

Donovan was silent for a moment. "Do you have a library card?"

"Of course." She was offended that he would even ask. "Do you?"

He nodded. "That's my turn-on."

"Library cards?" He had just taken kinky to a whole other level.

"Women who love to read."

"That's really bizarre." And incredibly interesting. "Why?"

"Women who can lose themselves in a book don't need me to entertain them." Donovan shrugged a shoulder. The sensation had Rose biting back a moan. "They can entertain themselves for hours. So when they choose to spend time with me, it's not because they're bored. I know it's because they really want to be with me."

Was he kidding? Who wouldn't want to spend time with Donovan Carroll? He was handsome, intelligent and infinitely intriguing. "We can't keep our noses buried in a book all the time."

"There's something very sexy about a woman when she's carried away in a book." His voice was soft and low, hypnotic. "Her love of reading shows she has a creative mind. She always has something to talk about."

His words seduced her. They brought to mind lazy, rainy afternoons, curled up on her love seat with a good book. Mysteries, fantasies, romance.

Her body relaxed. "What do you like to read?"

"I like variety. Fiction and nonfiction, mysteries, science fiction, adventure. I've even read romance. My only requirement is that the author be a good storyteller. What about you?"

He sounded too good to be true. "The same. I'm not particular. Just give me a good story."

"So we finally have something in common." He leaned his head back against her sofa and closed his eyes. "What a relief."

Rose chuckled. "Give it a rest, Van."

She sat up. Her eyes traced the clean line of his profile to the long, strong column of his throat. He really was a very handsome man.

Donovan's eyes flew open, startling Rose. She stared into their depths. They were a bright golden brown, surrounded by a rim of forest green. For a moment, she forgot she was curled up on his lap, talking about books.

"Your turn." His voice was low, husky, as though he didn't want anyone to overhear them.

"What?" she whispered back.

"What's your turn-on?"

Men who are turned on when they see a woman reading. She shied away from offering that answer, though. Maybe another time. "A sense of humor."

"Knock, knock." His eyes glowed brighter.

Donovan's fingers tunneled into her hair. He lifted his head as he brought her closer for his kiss. His lips touched hers and she forgot . . . everything. Her eyes fluttered closed. For the first time in a long time, Rose gave in to sensation. Donovan's lips were hot and firm, moving on hers. He took his time, tracing the shape of her mouth with his. The top. The bottom. Each corner. Over and over again.

152

Her body grew warm and restless. Soft and pliant. She melted against him. Donovan's arms wrapped around her, drawing her even closer. His body's heat radiated into hers, spreading from her abdomen out to her limbs. Her breasts. Desire was building. She hadn't felt this way in so long, if ever. She moved her hands, sliding them up and over his arms, feeling the strength in his biceps and shoulders. Delicious.

Donovan opened his mouth, and she let him in. His tongue stroked hers in a long caress. He tasted so warm and so good. Rose held him closer. Tighter. Donovan shifted and she ended up beneath him on the love seat. His weight pressed deliciously against her. The cushions gave way beneath. His hand slid up her side to close over her breast. Rose shivered. A pulse beat between her legs. Donovan molded her, stroked her. Rose shifted restlessly against him. He deepened their kiss, his urgency growing. Donovan lowered his head and moved his mouth over her cheek to her neck. His hips moved against hers. Rose's body flooded with heat and dangerous desire. Her body wanted what he offered her, but her mind was cautious. They weren't in a relationship. This wasn't about happily-ever-after. This was a verbal agreement with a start date and an end date. What would happen to them when this was over?

Rose's palms were gentle but firm against his chest. "Van. Stop."

His torso shook, then stilled above her. His body's heat wrapped her like a blanket. Donovan straightened, sitting up and away from her.

Rose swung her legs from his lap, then pressed against the opposite end of the love seat. "I'm sorry."

"So am I."

But what were they sorry for? Her body still throbbed. "It's a dangerous game we're playing. This relationship isn't real. We need to remember that." Rose winced at the thin breathiness of her voice.

"I know." Donovan scrubbed his hands over his face. "You're right."

"We need to get to know each other. But we can't cross the line." Rose drew a deep breath as her body continued to pulse.

"It's a fine line." Donovan pushed himself to his feet without looking in her direction. He started toward her door.

She followed him on unsteady legs. "Are we okay?"

Donovan stopped and turned to her. His eyes were still hot with desire. Rose felt herself sway toward him. She stepped back.

His expression was so serious. She hadn't seen that look since the night they'd worked together on the shelter's statement.

"We will be." He opened her door and disappeared into the afternoon.

Rose wasn't as certain they'd recover from today's experience. What happened would leave a lasting impression on them. She locked her door, then leaned against it. Good grief, had she made a mistake? She'd never considered the possibility that she'd be overwhelmed by a physical attraction to Donovan Carroll, although she should have. The man was too handsome for her peace of mind.

She pushed away from the door and returned to her living room. A quick glance toward her leather love seat made her pulse trip. She caught her breath. Rose moved on to her matching sofa. She sank onto the cushion, glaring across the room. She'd made a mistake. *Dammit!*

Donovan wasn't a good candidate for her fake boyfriend. And let's face it, he wouldn't make a very good real boyfriend, either. Rose had tried the handsome-player type with Benjamin. Look how that had turned out. Donovan was even better looking than her ex-fiancé. She couldn't survive another heartache, real or fake.

She dropped her head into her hands. *What am I going to do?*

"I need a new fake boyfriend." Rose sat at Lily's kitchen table later that afternoon. In a moment of desperation, she'd sent her sister a 9-1-1 text, asking if Lily was free to talk. She'd received an immediate reply: Come over; have brewed iced tea. Lily brewed the best iced tea.

Now, seated on the other side of the rectangular, honey-wood table, Lily regarded Rose for a long, silent moment. *Is she ever going to respond, or is she just going to sit there, staring at me as though I haven't said anything?*

"Did Van make a pass at you?" Lily's question caught Rose off guard.

"What makes you think something happened between us?" Rose crossed her legs. She wore the same black shorts and gray tunic she'd had on when Donovan had made his pass earlier. Her body grew warm.

"You wouldn't have whirled in here like a tornado if he'd only shaken your hand." Lily gave her a knowing look. "In fact, you wouldn't be here at all if you hadn't liked it."

"What? You're mistaken." Was it hot in the kitchen? Rose fidgeted on the smooth wooden chair. She took a long drink from her glass of iced tea. It was cool and refreshing, with a hint of lemon and chai.

"Am I?" Lily seemed skeptical. "Then why are you so anxious to replace Van?"

Rose took a calming breath. The air smelled of lemons. Lily must have just finished cleaning. "I want someone else to be my reunion date."

"I still don't think you need a fake boyfriend. You should go alone." Lily leaned back, crossing her legs. Her cotton shorts jumper was a swirling pattern of spring flowers. The shorts ended midthigh.

Why was Lily always so stubborn? Once she got an idea, she'd never let it go. She was so certain she was right all the time. She was just like . . . Rose.

"Lil, I told you, I won't go to the reunion alone while Ben attends with his pregnant wife. *I* should be the pregnant wife Ben takes to the reunion. He took that away from me."

"I'm sorry, Rosie." Lily reached across the table to squeeze Rose's forearm. "Honestly, I think Ben's wife saved you from making a serious mistake."

Rose sighed. "You and Iris never liked Ben."

"We tried to." Lily straightened, releasing

Rose's arm. "But you deserved better, someone who was more interested in you. Ben is very self-absorbed."

"You were right." Rose propped an elbow on the table and set her chin in her hand.

"I still don't know anyone who meets your fake boyfriend requirements, though. Maybe Iris can give you another name." Lily lifted her tall glass of iced tea and took a sip.

"I can't go back to Iris. She'd ask too many questions." Rose traced a line through the cool condensation on her glass.

"You mean like, why, after working with Van for more than six weeks, you now need to start over with someone else?"

"Yes, like that one." Rose gave her sister a hard look, cautioning her against that line of questioning.

Lily ignored the silent warning. "Rosie, what's going on?"

Rose hesitated. It wasn't that she didn't want to confide in her sister. She was afraid to face the truth. "I'm worried that if I spend more time with Van, I'll start confusing what's real and what's fantasy."

"Why would that be so bad?"

Rose's eyes widened. "I can't make the same mistake twice. I can't trust my feelings with someone like Van."

"Van isn't Ben." Lily leaned into the

kitchen table. "Van isn't a selfish, self-centered, egotistical user. From what I can tell, Van is the anti-Ben."

Rose winced. Her sister had just ruthlessly described Benjamin down to the bone. "Men like Van and Ben are players. They can't commit to one woman. And why should they when they can have *any* woman?"

"You're judging Van on his looks." Lily settled back on her chair, crossing her arms. "You're right — Van's very handsome man. And so is Ben. But they couldn't be any more different."

"What makes you so sure? You've spent one dinner with Van. That doesn't mean you know him."

"Can you see Ben volunteering for a homeless shelter?"

"No."

"And Van has real friends. I always had the impression that Ben was more tolerated than liked."

"I know." The more she thought about it, the more she wondered what she'd ever seen in Benjamin. He'd really had her fooled.

Lily continued. "This puts you right back where you started. You can either cancel your plans to attend your reunion —"

"I'm not going to do that."

"Go to your reunion alone —"

"I'm not doing that, either."

"Or attend with Van and risk having your heart broken again."

"Well, you're just a font of great ideas." Rose frowned. "I can't let that happen."

"Is getting back at Ben your main goal in attending your reunion?"

"I want him to see that I'm over him. That he doesn't matter to me anymore." More importantly, she wanted Benjamin to recognize that she *was* woman enough to attract and keep a man who, by the way, was even more attractive, successful and admired than Benjamin.

"If your only interest is revenge, you don't need to worry about falling in love." Lily stood, carrying Rose's glass and her own to the refrigerator.

"What do you mean?"

"You can't fall in love with one person while you're consumed with hate for someone else." Lily filled the glasses with more iced tea. She returned to the table, offering Rose her glass before reclaiming her chair.

Rose blinked. "I'm not obsessed with revenge, if that's what you're trying to say."

"Yes, you are." Lily projected supreme serenity as she sipped her drink. "You're stuck in time, Rosie. Until you let go of the

160

anger you're feeling toward Ben, you won't be able to move forward with anyone else."

Oh, yeah? Tell that to my heart. It seemed to be trying to move forward with Donovan. "Bringing a date to the reunion will help me let go of the past and move forward."

"I hope you're right." Lily didn't look convinced. "Will you stay with Van?"

"After listening to you review my options, I don't think I have a choice."

"I'm glad. He seems like the total package — looks, personality, integrity and more looks." Lily wiggled her eyebrows.

Rose silently agreed. "Besides, as you said, I've already invested six weeks with him. It seems pointless to start over now with someone else."

But can my heart survive the remaining six weeks until the reunion?

CHAPTER 9

Donovan recognized Rose's phone number on his cell phone's display on Monday morning. The question flashed across his mind: *Is she ending our arrangement?* When he hadn't heard from her for the rest of the weekend, he'd wondered whether this call was coming. Still, the thought of her dissolving their agreement sucked the breath right out of him. It wasn't all about the shelter's statement to the city council, either. He enjoyed spending time with her.

He swiped his thumb across his cellular phone display to accept Rose's call. He might as well get this over with. "Rose, hi. What can I do for you?"

"Good morning. Did you wake up on the wrong side of the bed?" Her voice poured down the line like rich Scotch and had the same effect on his system.

"More like the wrong bed." Donovan's lips curved in a reluctant smile. He recalled her office, its sterile environment and stark, bright furnishings. Did she still have the roses he'd bought her or had they faded?

"The question of right or wrong depends on your choice of bed, Mr. Carroll. Doesn't it?" She sounded almost pensive but Donovan also heard amusement. "It's possible you woke in exactly the right one."

Donovan imagined Rose pursing her lips in mock Puritan disapproval. His body tightened as he imagined himself tracing his tongue over her expression of disdain. Would the gesture make her smile — or would she take a bite out of him? "I guess it depends on who's making the decision."

Her low, husky laughter made his thighs flex. "Believe it or not, I didn't call to discuss beds with you. I called the city council. The members haven't discussed our statement yet."

"What's taking them so long?"

"They gave me the standard line about there being a lot to consider and the council having a full agenda."

Donovan pictured her rolling her eyes as she sat behind her immaculate white modular desk. "Thanks for following up with them."

"I told you Wednesday that I would."

"Not everyone remembers their promises." He was impressed with her all over again.

"It's my job." Her voice became brisk. "I wanted to give you that update. I'll give them another two weeks before following up again. Hopefully, they'll call me before then."

"The board's getting anxious for a response." Donovan also was becoming impatient. He hoped that if the council decided in the shelter's favor, Cecil would stop calling and emailing him for near-daily updates. But if the council decided against the shelter, that would open a different set of problems. He wouldn't worry about that now, though.

"I can understand the board's concerns. I'll let you know as soon as I hear anything. I promise. Have a —"

"I thought you were calling to end our agreement." Donovan sensed her surprise.

"I admit that I considered it." Her voice was low.

His hand clenched his cell phone. "What changed your mind?"

"We've already invested almost six weeks in our business agreement."

Donovan smiled at the trace of humor in her voice. "Yes, we have."

"But this is just pretend, Van. We have to

remember that. There's no reason for us to spend so much time together."

"We're walking a very fine line between fact and fiction." Donovan focused on the view outside his fifth-floor office: the vivid blue sky and vibrant green treetops that framed the concrete, metal and glass skyscrapers. "If you want to convince your former classmates that we're a couple, we need to come across as two people who care about each other."

"We'll have to rely on our acting skills." Rose exhaled. The sound caused Donovan to catch his breath.

"Are you still in love with Ben?"

"Good grief, no." Rose's response was instant and sharp. Donovan found great satisfaction in that. "My feelings for Ben died an unlamented death when I realized he'd been playing me for a fool."

"Your anger is understandable, but how long are you going to hold on to it? At some point, you have to leave the past in the past."

"I disagree. The past is always with us." Her voice hardened. "It shapes us. I'll never forget the lesson Ben taught me, and I never want to."

"What lesson was that?"

"Men can't be trusted."

Donovan's eyes widened. Hearing her

express those feelings made him wonder if he'd ever be able to reach her.

Why am I worried about that?

He sat up on his executive chair. "You'll have to at least pretend to trust me. We're supposed to be in love."

"As long as we both remember that we're just pretending. Goodbye, Van." She didn't wait for his reply.

Donovan set down his cell phone. That was going to be a problem, recognizing where the pretense ended and real feelings began. Saturday had felt a little too real for him.

"You've been unusually quiet today." Xavier walked into Donovan's office late Monday afternoon.

Donovan watched the finance executive settle onto one of the gray upholstered guest chairs in front of his desk. Seven weeks had passed since Xavier had broken up with his girlfriend. He seemed to be putting the unpleasant experience behind him. His confidence and sense of humor were returning. Good. But Donovan was curious; how much of Xavier's healing was due to time and how much of the credit belonged to Lily Beharie. The Beharie sisters were having quite an effect on the Anderson men.

166

"I've got a lot on my mind. I'm planning the sales campaign for our new games." Donovan glanced at the clock on his computer monitor. It was just after five. The day had disappeared in a flash.

"Have you heard from Rose?" Xavier settled his right ankle on his left knee. To the casual observer, the other man seemed relaxed, but Donovan sensed his friend's tension. What was causing it?

"The city council hasn't met to discuss the statement yet." Donovan tapped a couple of keys on his keyboard, then spun his chair forward to face Xavier.

"Government entities move on their own special clock." Xavier's tone was dry.

"It's amazing anything gets done." Donovan studied his friend's expression. Xavier had an amazing poker face. "What's on *your* mind?"

Xavier's onyx gaze seemed to reach into Donovan's mind. "After what Lauren did to me, I felt like a jackass."

"This isn't on you — it's on her." Donovan's temper sparked when he thought of the games Xavier's ex-girlfriend had played with the finance executive. With all of them.

"No, Van, it's on me. I made the mistake." Xavier's voice was firm as he accepted responsibility. "Believe me, it's a mistake I'll never repeat."

"We know."

"You, Ty, Mom and Uncle Foster helped me realize that I can't let that mistake define me. It's not who I am. It's a lesson I learned."

Why did Donovan have the sense Xavier was trying to send him a message? If that were true, his friend would have to be much more direct.

"I'm glad you realize that." Donovan hoped Xavier was in fact on the road to recovering from his horrible relationship experience. He and Tyler hadn't liked Lauren. Donovan suspected Kayla and Foster hadn't, either. They'd liked her even less after what she'd done to Xavier, Iris and their company.

"You should realize it, too."

"What do you mean?" Donovan frowned.

"Tell Rose about your childhood and the time you spent in the homeless shelter."

"We've had this discussion. I'm not going to do that, Xavier." Donovan's protective walls settled into position.

"The women who broke up with you because you spent a couple of months in a homeless shelter when you were a child were ignorant."

Donovan arched a brow at his friend's

harsh judgment. "It was more than a couple of months."

Xavier lowered his right foot onto the floor and leaned forward. "Those women don't define you, Van. You do. And with all you've accomplished, you've defined yourself very well."

Donovan stared blindly at the papers strewn across his desk. Xavier's words were powerful, but then so was Donovan's reluctance. "If my past doesn't define me, why do I need to tell Rose?"

"We can't forget the past. It's a part of who we are." Xavier spread his hands. As always, he had an answer for everything. "We can't rewrite it, and we shouldn't forget it."

Donovan wanted to take his friend's counsel, but there was a lot at stake — perhaps too much. His body tightened as he remembered the way Rose had felt in his arms. Her scent. Her taste. He inhaled deeply, filling his lungs to ease his tension. The scent of fresh coffee teased him even as he tried to hold on to the memory of Rose's fragrance, vanilla and spice.

"I don't know how far this thing with Rose will go." Donovan ran his right hand over his clean-shaven head. "I don't even know what to call it."

"Then don't call it anything." Xavier shrugged.

"You're full of answers today."

"It's not hard when the answers are obvious."

"I wish they were to me." Donovan snorted. "I'm still not ready to risk what might happen if Rose finds out about my past."

"I understand, but I don't think Rose will walk out on you. She needs you for the reunion."

Why did it bother him to have Xavier remind him of his bargain with Rose? He and Rose referred to their "relationship" as fake all the time. It shouldn't disturb him to have other people make the same observation.

But it did.

Donovan crossed his arms over his chest. "We only have another six weeks with each other. That's another reason not to bring up the past."

"You're right. But there's a really good reason to stop avoiding it."

"What?"

"If you don't define yourself to Rose, someone else will."

That realization didn't sit well with Donovan. He didn't want to risk some stranger telling Rose who he was. Whether they remained friends or became something more, *he* wanted to be the one who explained his past to her.

Donovan grabbed his project folder and started toward his office door late on Tuesday morning. His first stop would be Tyler's office for a product update before he continued on to his 11:00 a.m. meeting with his sales team. But before he got to his door, his cell phone buzzed. His caller identification recognized Medgar Lawrence's number. The longtime board member never contacted him during the day.

He accepted the call with an uneasy feeling. "Medgar, hi. How can I help you?"

"You can stop Boy Wonder from taking your job." Medgar's rough voice was thick with disgust.

"Cecil?" With his foot, Donovan nudged the stopper out from under his office door. He shut the door, then dropped onto one of the chairs at his small circular conversation table. "What's going on?"

"I'll give you the short version." Medgar blew an exasperated breath. "Last night, you sent the entire board an email update, explaining that the city council didn't have an update for your young lady."

"That's right." Although he hadn't referred to Rose as his "young lady."

"Boy Wonder copied your email and forwarded it to the board — minus you — claiming that, if he were in charge, we'd have a response by now. He also said some disparaging things about your lady's legal experience. Here, I'm forwarding the email to you now." Medgar sounded distracted as he went through the process of sending the email.

"I can't believe this." Donovan's temper sparked at the knowledge that Cecil had disparaged Rose. "What's the reaction been?"

"Mixed." Medgar snorted. "Our subcommittee knows he's a young upstart — that he's all fire and flash, no substance. But he's managed to snow the rest of the board." He snorted again. "I've often wondered about the IQ of some of our members."

Donovan withheld his verbal agreement with Medgar's suspicions about some of their colleagues. He'd witnessed the Cecil Effect himself during regular board meetings and other events. It was as though some members — all responsible, successful professionals in their own right — were under a type of spell. What was it about

Cecil that impressed some people beyond reason?

"If Cecil's the leadership they want, then I'm not in a position to get in their way." Although he wondered whether he'd be able to remain with the board under the leadership of someone as criminally clueless as Cecil Lowell.

"Then you'd better put yourself in the position. I told you, Boy Wonder is after your job."

"I'm not going to block the members' right to elect my successor when my term ends next October."

"That's what I'm trying to tell you, Van." Medgar spoke slowly. "This Gen Y baby isn't trying to wait until your term is over. He wants your job now, and he's planning a coup to take it."

Donovan froze. "He hasn't served on the board a full term, but he thinks he's qualified to be president?"

"Now you're getting it."

"Do any of the board members support him?"

"Quite a few. He talks a good game."

"I can't believe this." Donovan was tempted to let the board stew in their folly. But he couldn't. Some members might be willing to act rashly, but their work wasn't a game. Real lives were at stake.

"Read his email." Medgar's advice stopped the carousel of Donovan's thoughts.

Donovan checked his black wristwatch. It was a few minutes before 11:00 a.m. "I've got a meeting. I'll read it afterward."

"I'm sorry to interrupt you at work. But Salma, Kim and I want you to at least serve out your term."

"I appreciate that." Donovan stood, preparing to leave.

"What are you going to do?"

Donovan crossed to his door. "Like you said, I'm going to serve out my term."

"Have you had dinner?" Donovan showed up at Rose's door Tuesday evening. He hoped the bags of Mexican takeout he'd brought would get him into her house. The expression on her face told him he'd need more than hope.

Rose leaned against her doorjamb, arms crossed. "I thought we talked about this yesterday. We're not really dating."

"I know, but I wanted to see you."

Her gaze wavered. "You can't just show up, Van. It's not cute."

"But I come bearing gifts." He lifted the large paper bag of takeout. "It's from the restaurant where we had lunch. You liked the food."

A light breeze played with Rose's hair and carried the scent of wisteria from her garden. She was silent for several seconds, her gaze moving from his to the bag and back.

Finally, she stepped back. "You play dirty."

"All's fair." He crossed into her home and waited while she locked her front door.

Rose led him past her living room and into her kitchen. Donovan's gaze paused on her black leather love seat. The memory of the last time he'd visited still stirred his body. He was having a similar reaction to the sight of her tonight. Her dark brown blouse traced her slender curves, and her black shorts hugged her slim, well-rounded posterior. Her endlessly long, honey-gold legs were slim and well-toned. Even her bare feet were sexy. The whimsical pink nail polish seemed out of character for her strong, no-nonsense personality.

Rose's kitchen was smaller than Lily's, but Donovan felt more at home here. He liked the vivid blue walls framed with white hardwood. Silver curtains hung in the windows and French doors. They almost matched her kitchen appliances. Place mats sat in the center of her white wooden table.

Rose pulled plates from a cupboard and

silverware from a drawer. Together, they served the meal. Donovan remembered Rose liked the chicken fajitas. He'd bought himself enchiladas. They split the Spanish rice and pinto beans.

Anecdotes about their workday and current news carried them through most of dinner. It wasn't until he was helping Rose clean up after the meal that she circled back to the fact that he wasn't supposed to be there.

"Now, why are you really here?" Rose offered him another glass of iced tea before leading him back to her living room.

Donovan took the love seat alone. Rose settled onto the sofa. Her body language was clear: she wasn't taking any chances tonight.

"I wanted to talk with you." Now that he was here, the words wouldn't come. His mind was drawing a blank on what he needed to say and how he should say it.

"You could have called." Rose curled her long runner's legs beneath her.

Donovan's palm tingled with the need to caress her graceful calf. He lifted his eyes to hers. "I needed to tell you this in person."

"What's happened?" The concern in Rose's chocolate eyes made Donovan feel less isolated. It was reassurance that she had some feelings for him.

"Rose, I want you to know . . ."

"What?" she gently prodded.

"I was homeless. My father and I. For about a year and a half. When I was eleven." Donovan took a deep drink of his iced tea, then waited for Rose's reaction. His tension increased with every second of silence.

"Van, I know." Her tone was almost apologetic.

"You know?" Donovan frowned when she nodded confirmation. "How?"

"One of my classmates, Tasha Smalls, works with Whitley Maxwell."

Donovan winced at the mention of his former girlfriend. He drew a deep breath, then exhaled. "It really is a small world."

A smile eased the concern on Rose's lovely face. "Tasha didn't have any details. But she thought I should know."

"How long have you known?"

"She told me about four days ago."

Donovan did the math. Rose's friend had told her about his past the day before they'd made out on this very love seat. His muscles pulsed again. "What did you tell her?"

"I pretended that I already knew. I didn't want her to think we were keeping secrets from each other."

"I'm sorry. I probably should have told

you sooner."

Rose shrugged a shoulder. "We have a business arrangement. You're not under any obligation to share personal details of your life with me."

"I suppose not." Donovan stood to pace her living room. He took another long drink of iced tea.

"Tasha told me because she thought your being homeless even for a brief time in your childhood would matter to me. It doesn't."

"Are you sure?" He spoke over his shoulder.

"Positive. But I have to say you've really impressed me."

"Why?" Donovan turned away from her fireplace and faced her.

"Look at what you've accomplished." Rose spread her hands. Her eyes were wide with surprise. "You've already achieved a lot by becoming one of the top executives at a successful, international computer gaming company. And you're only in your thirties. You accomplished all that despite your disadvantaged background. Your parents would be very proud of you."

Donovan turned back to the fireplace. Her words had rocked him. He braced his hands on the mantel to keep himself upright. When he'd told the woman who'd professed to love him that he'd been homeless, she'd kicked him to the curb. But now the woman with whom he had a business relationship offered him words of encouragement and admiration.

He drew a deep breath to settle the chaos churning inside him. "I hope my parents would be proud. They were good people."

"May I ask what happened?" Rose was uncharacteristically tentative.

Donovan faced her, shoving his hands into the front pockets of his tan shorts. "My mother had cancer. It came as a shock to our family because she took really good care of herself. She exercised, ate healthy, never smoked. Still, she contracted cancer. And despite her regular health checkups, her doctor didn't discover the cancer until it was too late."

"I'm so sorry."

"So am I." Donovan cleared his throat. His mother had died twenty-five years ago. Still sometimes it hurt as if it was yesterday. "My father thought we had good health insurance, but it wasn't good enough. After two years of treatments, my mother died and we were left with a lot of debt."

Restless, Donovan moved away from the fireplace to continue pacing Rose's living room. "It was hard on my father, taking care of me and my mother. It was too much. He lost his landscaping business."

Rose gasped. "That's horrible."

"Yes, it was." Donovan turned away from Rose's sound system and walked toward her bay window. "It took a while, but with the help of strangers, my father was able to get back on his feet. Things were never the same after my mother died, though. They'd been high school sweethearts and very much in love." Donovan stopped and stared out the window at the gathering twilight.

He didn't hear her leave the sofa, but Rose's reflection appeared beside his in the window. She wrapped her arms around him from behind and rested her cheek on his back between his shoulder blades. The soft weight was comforting, healing.

"Your parents were very impressive people." Her words were just barely audible. "They would be proud of the man you've become, all that you've accomplished and of what you're giving back to the community."

It wasn't his imagination. He was falling in love with Rose Beharie — if he hadn't already fallen.

Donovan turned in her embrace. Rose dropped her arms and stepped back. Her chocolate eyes were soft with compassion, warm with admiration and bright with curiosity. His gaze sought her mouth. Her soft, pink lips parted slightly. His need to taste their fullness was like a fever. His muscles ached with the urge to pull her to him, lower his mouth to hers and drink her sweetness.

But it was the compassion in her eyes that kept him at a distance. When he kissed her — and he fully intended to kiss her again — he wanted to taste her passion, not her pity.

"Thank you." Donovan forced his legs to carry him past Rose and back to her fireplace.

"Is your experience the reason you volunteer with the homeless shelter?"

"Yes." Donovan met Rose's eyes over his shoulder. "But I don't know how much longer I'll be on the board."

"What would make you say that?" Rose stepped closer.

Donovan crossed his arms over his chest and faced her. "One of the junior members of the board is preparing to challenge my presidency. He and I have very different visions for the shelter. If the board agrees with his vision, I don't think I could stay."

"That would be a shame." She placed her hand on his bicep. "But whatever you choose to do, I know you'll make your parents proud."

Donovan gazed down into her beautiful eyes. What kind of man would make Rose Beharie proud? He needed to know because he wanted to be that man.

CHAPTER 10

Donovan stood at the podium in the Hope Homeless Shelter's community room on Thursday night. Medgar, Salma and Kim thought it had been a mistake to wait nine days before calling this special meeting of the board of directors. They'd argued the delay gave Cecil more time to persuade members to support him as an alternative to Donovan. Perhaps they were right. He was taking a calculated risk. Donovan wanted to finish his term. However, he needed to know where the other members stood. He wanted them to have the opportunity to consider their options. Did they share his vision for the shelter or did they find Cecil's ideas more attractive? He hoped tonight he'd have the answers to his questions.

"Good evening, and thank you for coming." Donovan waited for the other twenty-four board members to quiet down before he continued.

Cecil was seated in the front row. Medgar, Kim and Salma sat apart from him toward the center of the audience.

The best defense is a strong offense. How many times had his father reminded him of that?

Donovan rested his hands on the podium's smooth, cool wooden surface and held Cecil's gaze. "Some of you have a different goal for the shelter than I do. And you want to work toward that goal now. Isn't that correct, Cecil?"

The look of surprise that crossed Cecil's soft, round features would have been humorous if the situation wasn't so serious.

Cecil slid forward on his chair. "You're right. You and I disagree on several things, including the pawnshop. I believe that the area needs more businesses, not less."

Had Cecil been misrepresenting his position to the other board members? That wouldn't surprise him.

"I don't believe we need *fewer* businesses in the community. We need the *right* ones."

"And what would your definition of *right* be, Mr. President?" Cecil stood and looked around the room, drawing the other members' attention to him.

Donovan glanced toward Medgar, Kim

and Salma. They wore various expressions of disgust at Cecil's display. Kim rolled her eyes.

Their reaction restored his sense of humor. "I appreciate your asking that question, Cecil. My definition of the right type of business is one that gives back to the community. And I mean more than just during Operation Feed or United Way drives."

"All right, I'll bite." Cecil crossed his arms over his narrow chest. "Gives back how?"

"With good jobs and services that benefit our clients. We need businesses that maintain their property, and participate in the community instead of just draining money from it." Donovan considered Cecil's brash manner. Did he realize the importance of this debate?

"These are adult men and women." Cecil smirked. "Why are you so intent on coddling them?"

"It's fine for you to talk about coddling people, Cecil. How far from your home is the nearest pawnshop?"

"What does that have to do with anything?"

"Just take a guess."

"I have no idea."

"Is it five blocks, ten blocks?"

"I've never seen one in my neighborhood."

Cecil shrugged his narrow shoulders under his conservative black suit jacket.

"Really?" Donovan arched a brow. "Then someone's coddling you."

A murmur of agreement rolled across the room. Donovan glanced back toward Medgar, Kim and Salma. They smiled at him.

"I wouldn't be opposed to having a pawnshop move into my neighborhood." Cecil dropped his arms and glanced around the room.

Donovan sensed his opponent's growing agitation. "Then perhaps you could invite Public Pawn to open a location there instead of in the shelter's neighborhood."

A few chuckles interrupted their debate. Cecil flushed. "Maybe I will."

"For the record, I wouldn't be opposed to having a grocery store, convenience mart or pharmacy move into the vacant buildings near the shelter."

"Oh, ho!" Cecil threw his arms up. His grandstanding was an obvious effort to turn the tide back in his favor. "Now you want to pick and choose the types of companies that move into the neighborhood."

"Communities have been doing that for years." Donovan released the podium and stepped back. "You've put on a good show for this audience, Cecil. But this debate is not for entertainment value. The outcome of tonight's meeting will impact the community we're supposed to be serving and decide the vision for the shelter's future."

Cecil gave him a challenging smile. "Are you really going to do this?"

"Yes, I am. I won't single-handedly decide the direction the shelter should take. That's up to the board and I'm willing to let them have their say." Donovan glanced at Medgar, Kim and Salma. Their wide-eyed expressions of shock didn't bolster his confidence. "Do I have a motion for an emergency vote for president of the board?"

Cecil cocked his chin. "I move that an emergency vote for president of the board be held tonight."

Donovan nodded. "Do I have a second?"

Medgar raised his hand slowly. "I'll second the motion."

"The motion has been made and seconded." Donovan caught the eyes of several board members. "Is anyone opposed?" No one responded.

The murmurings were picking up again. Excitement swept the room. Board members looked at each other with surprise and anticipation. Donovan was disappointed to have come to a point where he had to defend his presidency, but if this was what the membership wanted, he would respect their wishes and the outcome of the vote.

He gripped the sides of the podium and leaned toward the microphone. "All those in favor of terminating the current presidency and holding elections for a new president of the board of directors, please raise your hand."

Cecil's hand rose before Donovan had finished speaking. That was to be expected. What he hadn't expected was the reaction of the rest of the board.

Rose answered her cellular phone as soon as she saw it was Donovan. "What happened?"

"The board voted against electing a new president." The relief in Donovan's voice was palpable.

"You're still president?" Rose was almost afraid to ask.

"I'm still president."

"I knew it! I knew it! I knew it!" Rose sprang from her black leather sofa. She jumped up and down, shouting with joy. "Oh, my word. That's fantastic. Congratulations!"

Donovan's chuckles grew into laughter — full, deep and appreciative. "Thank you."

"Tell me everything." Relief made Rose's

muscles weak. She collapsed back onto her sofa, listening intently while Donovan gave her an overview of the debate between him and Cecil.

"That would have been the perfect time to bow out of your position and just let Cecil take over."

"Yes, I guess it would have been."

"Then why didn't you?"

"I don't know."

"I think I do."

"Do you think you know me, Ms. Beharie, after only two months?" Donovan teased. The amusement in his voice sent shivers of pleasure up and down Rose's spine.

"I wouldn't go that far. But I think you didn't abdicate your presidency because the hero in you didn't want to leave your clients unprotected."

"I'm not a hero, Rose. But I admit the idea of Cecil leading the board and implementing his vision for the shelter makes my blood run cold. He's too young, not just chronologically. He doesn't have a clue about the vulnerability of disadvantaged communities."

Despite his protests, Rose knew Donovan was a hero. His words and actions proved it. But she'd keep his secret, if that's what he wanted. Let him protect his alter ego.

Rose stood from her sofa. "This calls for a celebration. What are you doing tomorrow night?"

"I don't know. What do you have in mind?"

"How about dinner, my treat?"

"Why, Ms. Beharie, are you asking me out on a date?"

Rose sensed a trap beneath Donovan's teasing tone. "No, this isn't a date. It's just a friendly celebration to commemorate your victory."

"Sounds like a date."

"Well, it's not." Rose wouldn't allow him to twist her intent. "Do you want to go out with me or not?"

"I will gladly accept your generous offer, which sounds a lot like a date."

"But isn't." Rose proposed the time and location. "I'll pick you up at your place."

"I don't think a woman's ever picked me up for a date before."

"Your record still stands because this isn't a date, stubborn man. Are we going to do this or not?" She was torn between exasperation and amusement. Amusement was getting the upper hand.

"I look forward to seeing you tomorrow night. Sleep well, Rose."

"You, too, Mr. President." Rose ended the call with Donovan's chuckle warm in her ear.

It was still early. She curled onto the sofa, setting the cellular phone on the coffee table in front of her. She was restless and excited, almost distracted with anticipation. Was she that excited over her upcoming night out with Donovan? More and more, Rose sensed the line blurring between fact and fantasy.

"You're serious about this." Donovan made the words a statement rather than a question. He climbed out of Rose's cobalt-blue BMW and closed the passenger-side door. He stood beside the car, staring across the parking lot at The Cheese Quartet.

"Of course, I'm serious." Rose studied her companion in amusement. Why hadn't he believed her when she'd told him she was taking him to a pizzeria? She tossed a grin at Donovan over her shoulder as she led him to the restaurant's entrance.

"A pizzeria." Donovan sounded disbelieving.

"It's not just any pizzeria." Rose spread her arms. "It's The Cheese Quartet. They have fabulous pizza."

"I'm sure they do." Donovan still sounded

dubious.

Rose mounted the sidewalk. Donovan's arm reached from behind her to pull open the entrance door. She looked up to thank him, then looked away before she could get lost in his wicked hazel gaze.

Minutes later, Rose trailed their host to a booth in a quiet section of the restaurant. Donovan followed her. She gazed around the crowded dining area. The wood trim framed stenciled musical notes interspersed with vibrant, stylized sketches of musicians and singers who were from Ohio, including John Legend, Macy Gray and Chrissie Hynde. The young man offered them menus, then left them on their own.

"I'm giving you fair warning — I don't like a lot of toppings on my pizza." Rose opened the menu to view her choices.

"I do." Donovan didn't sound prepared to back down.

Rose watched him closely. "What do you think about this place?"

"It's nice." He took in the decor with an expression of appreciation. "But it's not very romantic."

"I told you, this isn't a date."

"I got that impression when you showed up at my house in your denim shorts and strappy sandals." The look in his eyes, the tone of his voice made her body overheat.

Rose broke eye contact and dived back into her menu. It hadn't changed much since the last time she'd been here several months prior. "You would've understood this was just a celebration if you'd listened when I explained that over the phone last night."

"Spoken like a true girlfriend." His voice rumbled with laughter. "This just isn't what I imagined when you invited me to dinner."

"What had you expected?" Rose looked up. She was really curious.

"Something more upscale. You're too elegant for a pizza joint."

Rose stilled. "Is that the way you see me — elegant, cool, untouchable?"

"I believe I showed you a couple of weeks ago that I find you anything but untouchable." His voice lowered until its sound strummed the muscles of her lower abdomen. Steam swirled in his hazel eyes.

Rose forced herself to maintain eye contact. "Then why can't you picture me eating pizza?"

"I guess I need to get to know you better."

How do we always end up right back there?

Rose started to reply when a familiar voice called her name.

"Rose, I thought that was you. What a coincidence." Maxine materialized beside their booth with an attractive man.

Panic! "Maxine, what are you doing here?"

"Isiah and I came to have dinner. When I saw you, we headed straight for your table." Her friend gestured toward the tall, handsome man standing behind her. "Rose Beharie, my fiancé, Isiah Russell. Isiah, Rose is one of the legal ladies I have dinner with once a month."

Isiah stepped forward to offer Rose his hand. "It's good to meet you, Rose. Maxine has told me a lot about her law school friends."

Rose swallowed her dread. "It's very nice to meet you, Isiah."

Rose sent a distressed look in Donovan's direction. She read the message in his eyes: *See? Maxine told her fiancé all about you, but I didn't know she existed.*

Rose felt about three inches tall. She smothered a groan and turned her attention back to Maxine. The silence sounded like inevitability. It was apparent her friend was prepared to wait all day for an introduction to Donovan Carroll of Anderson Adventures. Maxine had made it very clear that she was a big fan of his company's computer games.

194

Rose took a deep breath, drawing in the scent of cheese and spices. "Maxine Ellerson and Isiah Russell, my . . . boyfriend, Donovan Carroll."

Donovan's eyes laughed at her as he rose to his feet. He stepped out of the booth to greet her friends. "It's a pleasure to meet both of you."

"Mr. Carroll." Maxine held on to Donovan's proffered hand. "Isiah and are a big fans of your company's games. Osiris' Journey has blown our minds. It takes gaming to a whole other level."

"Thank you. Please call me Van." Donovan grinned. "I'll be sure to share your enthusiasm with Ty Anderson."

Wide-eyed, Maxine turned to Rose and mouthed, "Ty Anderson."

"Van, it's good to meet you." Isiah's greeting was more understated. "Great job with the game."

"Thank you. I appreciate that." Donovan released the other man's hand. He took a step back and gestured toward the booth he'd just vacated. "Why don't you join us?"

Rose's eyes flared. Had he just . . . ?

"We'd love to. Thank you." Maxine slipped into the booth. Isiah followed her.

Rose scooted over to let Donovan sit beside her. She gave him a look that promised retribution. He responded with a smile that professed his innocence.

"Are you two going to the reunion in September?" Isiah shared a look between Rose and Donovan.

"Yes, we are." Donovan cupped Rose's hand as it lay on the table between them.

Rose looked at his hand on hers. It was broad and strong. His fingers were long and elegant. His skin was warm and just a little rough against hers. She lifted her eyes to his. Donovan squeezed her hand and gave her an encouraging nod. Was this part of their performance?

"That's good news." Isiah's smile was relieved. "I was afraid I wouldn't know anyone at the reunion other than Maxine."

Rose could see the appeal Isiah had for Maxine. He was handsome, fit and appeared to be humble. His pale blue polo shirt and beige cargo shorts enhanced his neat, conservative appearance. His close-cropped hair shaped his square head. His wire-rimmed glasses were subtle on his broad, blunt features.

Maxine was the perfect foil for Isiah's quiet, conservative appearance. She'd accessorized her vibrant red-and-gold peasant top with chunky silver jewelry.

Donovan squeezed Rose's hand again. "If

our ladies have to attend reunion events without us, we'll find a TV and turn on a game."

"And if the events are boring, your ladies will be joining you." Rose's voice was dry.

"Amen to that." Maxine chuckled.

Donovan held Rose's eyes. "Maybe this reunion won't be so bad."

Rose's cheeks heated under Donovan's open look of admiration. Benjamin had never looked at her that way. Her body had never responded to her ex-fiancé's gaze as fervently as it reacted to Donovan's attention.

The arrival of their server interrupted Rose's musings. The young man took their drink orders. Rose and Maxine ordered iced teas with lemon. Donovan and Isiah requested sodas.

Donovan's attention returned to the menu once their server disappeared. "We were debating toppings before you joined us."

"I like everything on my pizza." Isiah grinned.

Donovan inclined his head. "I can see we're going to get along."

"You two can share your heartburn-on-a-crust." Maxine waved a hand between Isiah and Donovan. "Rose and I will have our reasonable toppings."

Rose nodded. "That's a plan I can live with."

As the evening aged, Rose relaxed and enjoyed the company and conversation. Topics ranged from Anderson Adventures' creative genius in the computer gaming industry, to the schedule for Rose and Maxine's reunion weekend. They laughed and conversation hopped as though they'd all been friends for years. Afterward, Rose drove Donovan home.

She pulled onto his driveway, turned off the engine and shifted to face him. "I had a really nice time tonight."

"So did I." Donovan's voice was low in the car. He'd adjusted the front passenger seat to accommodate his long legs. "I like your friends."

"They really like you." A burst of pride filled Rose with that realization. She studied Donovan's home in the gathering dusk. His neighborhood in the Short North area was so quiet. They could be the only people for blocks. "Thank you."

"For what?" Donovan's bewilderment seemed genuine.

"Being the perfect pretend boyfriend." He'd been everything she'd wanted her fake boyfriend to be: courteous, charming, interesting and attentive.

He'd been especially attentive. With every touch and look, he'd made her feel special and cherished. The deep scar tissue that had remained after Benjamin's betrayal was starting to ease away. Rose had a moment's panic. What would happen when reunion weekend was over? Everything would be fine as long as she remembered that this was all make-believe.

"Thank you for pretending with me." Donovan shifted on his seat to face her. He seemed so close in the quiet confines of her car. She could feel his body's warmth. Smell his clean, fresh scent. "Do you want to come inside?"

She was tempted. Oh, was she ever. Then she read the question in his eyes. "We don't have to pretend anymore, Van. We're alone."

"I'm not pretending, Rose. You're a very beautiful, intelligent and interesting woman. I'd like to get to know you better. If the time we spend together benefits our playacting, then that's icing on the cake."

That kind of approach was fine for now. Tempting, even. But what about the long term? What would happen when the playboy met the real Rose Beharie and realized she couldn't hold his interest beyond her reunion weekend? She already knew the answer to that. He'd move on and she'd be left to pick up the pieces. Again. *No, thank you.*

"It's getting late." Rose tugged her eyes free of his mesmerizing gaze and straightened on her seat. "I should go home."

"All right." Donovan gave her a curious look. "What are you doing tomorrow?"

Rose's mind wiped clean. *Make something up.* "I'm not sure yet." *Stupid. Stupid. Stupid.*

"Then I have an idea." Donovan smiled. "Come by my place and I'll make you dinner."

"We've had dinner." *Apparently, my mind is still shooting blanks.*

"I owe you a meal."

The memory of their joint family dinner made Rose smile. "Actually, you *and* your friends owe my sisters and me dinner."

"All right." Donovan nodded. "You *and* your sisters are invited to my place tomorrow, and Ty, Xavier and I will cook dinner."

Caught off guard, Rose threw back her head and laughed. "Don't you think you should check with your friends before you commit them to cooking dinner for six?"

"Eight." Donovan's eyes searched her face. "I'm inviting Foster and Kayla, as well."

More gales of laughter. She could just imagine the looks on Tyler's and Xavier's faces when Donovan told them his idea. "And you expect them to plan and cook this feast in less than twenty-four hours? Suppose *they* have plans?"

Rose thought a flash of heat had brightened Donovan's hazel eyes before he lowered his eyelids. He shifted back on his seat, increasing the space between them. "They don't."

Rose gave him a skeptical look. Considering the long, hard hours Tyler and Iris worked during the week, she was pretty sure they had plans to spend the entire weekend together. Alone.

She glanced toward his house again. "Can your dining table seat eight?"

"Good point. We may need Kayla's home for that." Donovan frowned. "Just tell me you'll come. We'll work out the logistics later."

"Are you kidding? I wouldn't miss this for the world, and I'm sure my sisters wouldn't, either." She'd tell Lily and Iris in person. She couldn't wait for their reactions. "And Kayla can't help."

"Deal. We'll see you then." Donovan started to let himself out of the car.

Rose placed a hand on his shoulder to detain him. "And you can't pass off some restaurant's food as your own."

Donovan looked at her hand, then lifted his gaze to hers. Rose dropped her hand. She was scalded by the heat swirling in his hazel eyes. Her body warmed in response. With just a touch and a look, he'd made her question denying her desires.

Donovan's voice broke his spell. "Anderson Adventures men don't need to cheat. We strategize." Then he was out of her car and walking up the drive that led to his front steps.

Rose regarded Donovan's broad shoulders and trim waist covered by a cabernet-colored short-sleeved crew, and the way his gunmetal-gray cargo shorts fit his glutes. His parting comment echoed in her head: they don't cheat; they strategize. Rose shivered as she started her car and backed out of Donovan's driveway.

Why did she have the feeling his words were a warning meant for her?

CHAPTER 11

"You have a lovely home." Rose stood with her sisters in the entryway of Kayla Cooper Anderson's house. The mahogany flooring threw the ivory walls into sharp relief. The pink-and-silver marble trim was an elegant accent.

"Thank you, dear." Kayla escorted Rose and her sisters down the narrow hallway to her living room. "I believe your home is your sanctuary. This is where you should treat yourself."

Kayla's living room continued the pink-and-silver theme that she'd introduced in her entryway. Rose had an impression of bright ivory walls, fluffy silver furniture and a warm rose carpet before being distracted by the room's occupants.

The four Anderson Adventures men stood as the women entered the room. Rose's tongue stuck to the roof of her mouth. How she wished she had a camera to preserve this tableau of masculine appeal. The men wore tailored slacks and casual shirts in dark colors. Donovan's amethyst shirt made his hazel eyes glow.

"You guys look great." Iris's enthusiastic words were an understatement. "It's a good thing Lily had us dress up."

Iris's lipstick-red tank dress bared her calves. Lily's mint-green lace shift skimmed her hourglass figure. In her copper cap-sleeve sheath, Rose felt a little like a prickly cactus among colorful poppies.

"Good for Lily." Kayla put an arm around Lily's shoulders. The two were almost the same height. "But we still would have fed you."

"Dinner should be ready soon." Foster stood beside Kayla. "We're happy you could join us. Kayla and I were sorry to have missed the first family dinner."

Rose smiled at Foster and Kayla. How reluctant had they really been to skip the first dinner? Reading their body language, Rose had the feeling Foster and Kayla had been glad "the kids" were otherwise engaged that evening. Did Donovan, Tyler and Xavier know?

Tyler stepped forward to kiss Iris's cheek. "You look beautiful."

"Thank you." Iris glowed. "You look very

handsome."

Rose was distracted by the expression of pleasure on her sister's face. She jumped when someone claimed her hand. Looking up, she found Donovan beside her.

"You're beautiful." His words were meant for her ears only.

"So are you," she whispered back.

"I'm experiencing a lot of firsts with you." Donovan grinned. "No one has ever called me that."

Rose blushed. She needed to change the subject. "So you guys pulled it off. I'm impressed."

"It was a piece of cake — once Ty and Xavier stopped cursing me." Donovan gave her a rueful smile.

Tyler tucked Iris against his side. "I hadn't expected to spend my Saturday morning doing emergency grocery shopping."

"Uncle Foster was a great help." Xavier wandered forward to stand beside Lily.

Rose exchanged a knowing glance with Iris.

"Dinner smells wonderful." Lily smiled her appreciation.

Kayla dropped her left arm from Lily's shoulders. She linked her right arm with Foster's, then gave Rose, Lily and Iris a conspiratorial smile. "Let's move into the dining room so the men can serve us."

Dinner was excellent: broiled chicken tenders, Spanish rice and asparagus spears. Dessert was apple pie à la mode. But again, it was the company and conversation that made the meal memorable. Foster sat at the foot of the table with Tyler and Donovan on either side of him. Kayla was at the head of the table with Xavier on her right and Lily on her left. Rose and Iris had the table's two middle seats.

Rose was impressed. "Did you men honestly make all of this without any help from Kayla?"

"I wasn't even informed of the menu. This was a complete surprise." Kayla chuckled. "They even cleaned up after themselves. My kitchen is spotless."

Iris forked up more apple pie and vanilla ice cream. "I'm impressed with the meal and how quickly you pulled it together. I don't think I would've managed this."

"Now, we don't want to give them too much credit." Kayla winked in Lily's direction. "Women have been doing this for years and with much less help. But it does show how well these young men work together and why Anderson Adventures will continue to be successful."

Xavier shook his head. "Mom has a way

of bringing everything back to the company and its future."

"Kayla makes a good observation." Lily smiled. "You're able to handle tough challenges so well because you handle them together. That includes everything from the situation with Osiris' Journey earlier this year to this last-minute home-cooked meal for eight. You can do that not just because you're friends, but because you're family. You don't just love each other — you like each other."

Rose was struck by Lily's words. That's exactly how she felt about her sisters. She didn't only love them; she liked the hell out of them. They'd always been her guiding lights and her pillars of support. And she relied on them even more since the death of their parents. The Beharie sisters had a lot in common with the Anderson Adventures men.

"Very well said, Lily." Foster lifted his glass of lemonade toward her. "I knew the first time I met you that you understood the importance of family."

"I wish my parents had met you." Donovan looked from Kayla to Foster. "I wish they'd met all of you. I'm not a blood relative but you make me feel like a part of your family."

"That's because you are." Kayla leaned into the table as though to emphasize her words.

"You're like the irreverent cousin who turns every family event into a party." Xavier grinned down the table toward Donovan.

Laughter rose from the table, lightening the conversation again. Once dessert was over, the women cleared the table and loaded the dishwasher, much as the men had done after the Beharie sisters had hosted dinner.

Iris lingered behind with Tyler while Lily stood talking with Foster, Kayla and Xavier. Donovan took Rose's hand and drew her outside to the front porch. The evening was warm. A gentle breeze ruffled the nearby bushes and carried the scent of roses from Kayla's garden.

Rose stood in the shadows of the porch beside Donovan. The sole lightbulb traced the chiseled lines of his classically handsome face. "Thank you again for the lovely meal. The Anderson Adventures leadership team knows how to plan a social event."

Donovan flashed his million-dollar smile, the one advertising agencies would kill for. "We can handle the smaller celebrations. For the big events, we call in your sister."

"Thank you." Rose appreciated the compliment.

"The Andersons are good people." Donovan glanced back at the house. "Like I said, I think my parents would have liked them a lot."

"My parents would have liked them, too." Rose met Donovan's eyes. "I hope I'm not being too personal. But I was wondering, did your father ever remarry?"

"No, he didn't." Donovan's smile was soft with memories. "My mother was the one true love of his life. He said after he experienced that, he didn't want to settle for anything less."

"That's beautiful." Rose's heart melted. "Your father was a romantic."

Donovan chuckled. "I guess he was."

"He was a good role model." Impulse lifted Rose's hand to cup his cheek. "A hero, just like his son."

"I'm not a hero." Donovan lowered his voice.

"That's how I see you."

"I'd rather you saw me like this." Donovan closed what little space remained between them. He lowered his mouth to Rose's and took her breath away.

How could she have denied herself another taste of him for so long? He might ultimately prove to be bad for her but her body craved him. He was like another piece of chocolate or that second slice of pie. His taste was heaven going down but she'd pay for it later. Donovan's lips moved on hers, nibbling and sucking them until they parted in welcome. His tongue swept in, bold and demanding. Feeding her fantasies. Stoking her desires. His arms wrapped around her, drawing her tight against him. His hard torso pressed against her breasts. His hips were firm against her. His hand lowered to cup her derriere, holding her close to make her aware of his arousal. Rose moaned into Donovan's mouth. A wild and reckless hunger heated her blood. It rushed through her veins and burned in her belly. Her knees were weak. Rose slid her hands over his chest. She drilled her fingers into his shoulders to steady herself.

Donovan's lips released hers. He trailed kisses down the side of her neck and up again. He nibbled her jawline, then whispered in her ear. "I'm not a hero, Rose. I'm just a man. But I'd never hurt you. You can trust me." He shared one last kiss before he released her and went back inside the house.

What just happened?

Rose's legs shook. Her body throbbed. Her underwear was damp. She stumbled

210

across the porch to lean against the attached garage wall. She took deep breaths to try to calm her body. When that didn't work, she took several more. What had happened? All Donovan had done was touch and kiss her. But it was the way he'd touched her and the way he'd kissed her that made her want to strip off her clothes and wrap her naked thighs around him. *That's* what had happened.

He'd kissed her and made her realize that she wanted him. All of him: the playboy, the hero, the messy executive and every version of him in between. But like every decadent dessert, Donovan Carroll would come at a cost. How high was that price — and was she able to pay it?

"I have in my hand the response from the Columbus City Council to the position statement from the Hope Homeless Shelter." Rose crossed the threshold into Donovan's home Thursday evening. It was a struggle to contain her excitement. "It's an email message. The official letter should arrive tomorrow or next week."

"Don't march around waving it like a flag." Donovan closed and locked his front door. He turned to Rose, extending his hand. "Tell me what it says or give it to me so I can read it."

"Do you want me to read it to you?" She bounced on her toes. His impatience made her want to delay the announcement longer.

"Rose." His voice was a warning.

"All right. All right." Rose lowered the printed message, holding out her hand, palm up. "The gist of it is . . . you won. The city will decline Public Pawn's request to locate one of its stores in the shelter's neighborhood."

"Are you serious?" Donovan stilled. His smile was uncertain.

"Of course I'm serious." Rose crossed to him, handing over the sheet of paper. "I wouldn't joke about something like this."

Donovan read the email himself. A sexy grin curved his full lips and showcased his perfect white teeth. "I can't believe it."

"What do you mean, you can't believe it?" She playfully punched his shoulder. "I can believe it. Our argument was sound and reasoned, so of course, we would prevail. Heroes always do."

Donovan's beautiful hazel eyes were bright with joy. It vibrated from him in waves. "If I'm a hero, then so are you. I couldn't have done this without you."

"Yes, you could have. You just would've

had to come out of pocket for the billable hours."

Donovan threw back his head and laughed, making Rose's toes curl in her sensible black pumps. "This is fantastic. We have to celebrate." He crossed the room with long restless strides.

"We can start by calling Cecil Lowell." Rose turned, keeping track of Donovan.

"Cecil?" Donovan paused, frowning at her. "Why would we call him?"

"He didn't think we'd win."

"I think he didn't want us to win." A smile chased away Donovan's confusion. "But that's all right. Everyone's entitled to his — or her — opinion."

An impressive reaction. "You're a good person, Van. Most people would want to rub this victory in Cecil's face."

"Is that what you'd do?"

"Maybe." Rose shrugged. "Probably."

Donovan chuckled again, causing the muscles in her lower abdomen to shimmy and shiver. "I need to let the subcommittee, then the board know."

"I'll forward the email to you." Rose crossed to him. "Then you can forward it to them. When the letter arrives in the mail, I'll keep a copy, then give the original to you."

"Thank you." Donovan still sounded dazed.

"Congratulations."

"To both of us." Donovan pulled her into his arms.

What he'd intended to be a friendly, congratulatory gesture soon heated into something more. His body was so hot and hard against hers, and his scent was an aphrodisiac.

Donovan's head was spinning. He loosened his embrace on Rose and looked down into her chocolate eyes. He read confusion and desire in them.

"Rose." He heard the yearning in his whisper.

Her eyes continued to search his face. He didn't know what she was looking for. If he did, he'd give it to her. Anything. Everything. He wanted her that much. But not just for her body, as sexy and desirable as she was. He also was attracted to her heart. It was big enough to share. Her mind was quick and curious, and her laughter gave him a hard-on. He also liked the way she saw him. She thought he was a hero and that made him want to be one.

Donovan lowered his head to kiss her. His movement was slow and deliberate, giving

Rose plenty of time to reject him, if that's what she wanted to do. He prayed that she didn't. He needed to hold her. Wanted to kiss her. Burned to love her. It was August 20, only four weeks until the reunion. He was running out of time to persuade her to turn their make-believe relationship into their own fairy-tale romance.

"Rose," he whispered again, right before his lips touched hers.

Heat rushed through his veins. She tasted so sweet. Felt so soft. Smelled so good. Donovan pressed his mouth to hers. He stroked his tongue across the seam of her mouth. Rose's lips parted, letting him in. He slid his tongue inside, stroking her here, caressing her there. Rose moaned into his mouth. Donovan tightened his embrace. She pressed her body against him and deepened their kiss.

Is she letting me know that she wants me, too? Please, God, let it be yes.

Donovan braced himself, then took a step away from her. He kept his grip on Rose's slender upper arms and waited for her to open her eyes and focus on him.

"Rose, honey, I want you. But is this what you want?"

Rose raised her hand to cup the side of his face. "Yes, Van, I want to make love with

215

you." Her voice was slow and clear. There was no mistaking her message.

Donovan closed his eyes as his body shook with desire. Rose braced her hands on his chest and kissed him. Donovan's muscles contracted. A rush of need swept through him, faster and hotter than anything he'd ever felt before. He'd wanted her for so long and so badly. Without breaking their kiss, Donovan swept her into his arms and carried her up the steps. At the top of the staircase, he turned right into his bedroom. He crossed to the foot of his king-size bed and released Rose's long legs.

She made quick work of stripping off his green T-shirt. Rose stopped briefly to caress his chest. Her hands were soft and hot against his skin. Donovan reached for her, but she shook her head.

"I want to finish what I started." She reached for the waistband of his khaki shorts. With her chocolate eyes on his, she lowered the zipper and let his clothing fall to the floor. She stepped back. Her voice was husky. "You're amazing. Even better than I'd imagined."

"You pictured me in my underwear?" Donovan gave her a curious smile.

"Maybe." Rose flushed.

"That makes two of us." He wished he'd

known that. Donovan stepped forward and released the four silver buttons on Rose's black shirtdress. "Now it's my turn to see how closely fantasy matches up with reality."

He had no doubt the reality of her body would blow his fantasy out of the water. He released the belt from her waist and dropped it to the floor. Rose kicked off her pumps. Holding his gaze, she caught the hem of her dress and pulled it over her head. Donovan stilled. He sucked in a breath and held it. Rose had been hiding her more colorful clothing beneath her staid black, brown, gray and bronze outfits.

Donovan's gaze slid over her matching hot-pink, barely-there lace underwear. He groaned. "No one could have fantasized about this." He stepped forward. "Rose, you're gorgeous."

He took the weight of her right breast in his left hand. He stroked his thumb over her nipple through her lace demicup bra. Rose's sharp gasp made his body heat. Donovan pulled her into his embrace and kissed her. Hard. He cupped the firm, rounded curves of her bottom and pressed her against his throbbing muscle. With his free hand, he released her bra, letting it drop to the floor. Her bare breasts felt wonderful against his chest. Donovan's blood was on fire for this woman. She tasted like heaven and felt like paradise. Her scent, vanilla and spice, was making him crazy. He led her to his bed, then fell onto the mattress, pulling her on top of him. They broke apart at the bounce. Rose looked up at him. The steam in her chocolate eyes echoed the heat building inside him.

"Tell me you have condoms." Her body was so still, waiting for his response.

"I do. Right there." Donovan jerked his head toward his nightstand. But if he hadn't had them, he would have driven naked to the store to get them.

Her smile was wicked relief. She moved down his body and removed his underwear, then returned to his erection.

"Your skin is so hot." Her voice was low as she touched him. She stroked him from root to tip, front and back. "I think you're ready for me."

Donovan gritted his teeth against the torturous caress. Watching her touch him as she lay practically naked between his legs, he thought he'd come any second.

"Come here, temptress." Donovan reached forward and pulled her on top of him. "We'll play your game later. Right now, I need you."

■ ■ ■ ■

He needs me. Rose smiled. The desire glowing in his hazel eyes confirmed it. She rolled
off Donovan to shed her underwear.

Then he settled his body on top of her.
"Am I heavy?"

"Just right." She brought his head down
for a kiss. She loved kissing him. The way
he felt. The way he tasted. What he did with
his tongue.

Donovan shifted his leg, using it to make
room for himself between her thighs.

Rose broke their kiss. "Condom."

He looked down at her. His eyes were
warm with promise. "We're not there yet."

Rose frowned. She was damp. Her nipples
were hard. How much further was there to
go?

Then she felt him reach for her. He held
her gaze as her eyes widened. His long,
nimble fingers stroked their way into her
folds. Rose's lids lowered as her body filled
with pleasure.

Donovan lowered his head to whisper
beside her ear. "That's it. Relax for me,
Rose. I need you."

Oh, my goodness. I hope you always do.

Rose's legs trembled. She spread them

wider, giving Donovan better access to her. She sensed him watching her but didn't care. Desire flooded her body. With every stroke of his finger, Rose's muscles tightened, pulling harder and harder, going deeper and deeper. Growing in intensity. Her hips pumped, chasing the craving. Rose's lips parted in a gasp at the sweet pleasure-pain. Her legs tensed and her muscles stiffened. Then her body burst as pleasure exploded inside and over her. Rose threw her arms around Donovan and held him tight.

"Oh, my." Rose gasped for breath. "I'm so sorry. I came too quickly. It's been a little while. I'm so sorry."

"Don't apologize." Donovan laid a finger over her lips. "You were beautiful."

Donovan shifted down her body. He covered her chest and shoulders with kisses. Over and over he repeated, "So beautiful." Under his attention, her body began to relax again.

"You're so beautiful, Rose."

She gave him a dreamy smile. "And you're so handsome. And talented. Magic."

Donovan drew her breast into his mouth. Rose gasped. She cupped the back of his clean-shaven head to urge him closer. He suckled her deeper. Rose dampened. She bit her lower lip as the pleasure intensified. Her legs moved restlessly. Donovan's teeth grazed her nipple. Her back arched. He stroked her tip with his tongue. Her hips pumped. Donovan released her right breast to minister to the other. Rose squeezed her eyes shut.

"Van, come in me now. Come in me now." She'd never begged before, but she was willing to now.

"Soon, Rose. I promise you. Soon." Donovan continued to trail kisses down her torso. He licked her navel and bit the side of her hip.

Rose's hips lifted. She wanted him in her. She needed to feel him. She had to —

Donovan cupped her hips, rose onto his knees and brought her to his mouth. Rose gasped at the unexpected caress. Donovan's tongue was rough against her spot as he stroked her. Rose pressed her head back against the pillow — hard — as her body shook with sensation. He kissed her. Licked her. His tongue moved in and around her. Rose clutched the bedsheets in her fists as her body rocked with pleasure. Her nipples hardened, and her thighs tensed. Her blood rushed in her ears. Her body was covered with sweat. Her muscles stretched tight until they burned. She pressed herself harder against him, opening wider. And then it happened. The thunder of completion rolled through her again. Wave upon wave of explosions. Her body shivered, then shook. She grabbed the pillow beside her, pressed it to her face and screamed.

Finally, Rose caught her breath. She removed the pillow from her face. Donovan was seated on the side of the bed, preparing to put on a condom.

"Let me." Rose rolled to her knees and extended her hand for the packet. Her body was satiated, languid and loved.

"Thanks." He knelt on the bed in front of her.

"You have amazing self-control." She unrolled the condom on his erection, using the task to avoid looking into his eyes.

"I wanted to love you." He buried his fingers in her hair and brought her closer for his kiss.

Amazingly, Rose was becoming aroused. Again. She pulled away from his kiss. "Now let me love you, hardworking man."

Donovan's eyes flared with hunger. Rose nudged him onto the mattress, then straddled him. She took her time loving his torso with licks and kisses. A touch here. A nip there. His big body shook between her thighs. From her. She was the focus of his desire. Rose felt sexual and powerful as she'd never felt before.

She straightened and guided him to the entrance to her core. Donovan shut his eyes hard as she slowly lowered herself onto his erection. He felt so good, pushing into her. Rose's nipples pebbled. Her muscles hummed. What was it about this man that had her on hair-trigger arousal?

Donovan's big hands gripped her thighs. Rose squeezed and stroked his muscle with her body. She picked up her rhythm and Donovan rocked with her. He panted and pressed his head deeper against his pillow as though struggling to hold on. Rose held him tighter to push him a little closer to the edge. She arched her back, clenching her muscles around him. Then he touched her. All of her senses collected in that one spot where his thumb rubbed her. He shifted his hips to deepen the pressure on her. Rose went wild. Her body convulsed as the climax shot through her. And with three powerful thrusts, Donovan followed.

Rose collapsed onto him, and he held her tight. She heard his heartbeat galloping in his chest. Hers was doing the same. She kissed the spot above his heart, then laid her cheek against his chest. Donovan kissed the top of her head, and then rested.

This was loving. Rose sighed much later as she spooned against Donovan on his king-size bed. She was exhausted. Instead of leaving now, she'd get up early to drive home and dress for work.

She'd never imagined she'd have three orgasms in one night. Perhaps Benjamin had been too sated from those other women to even try. With Benjamin, they'd had foreplay, then they'd had sex and afterward, they'd go to sleep. Rose had been satisfied. But she'd never been loved. Not like this. And she'd never be loved like this again. She pressed her face against her pillow and let the tears flow.

CHAPTER 12

On Friday afternoon, Donovan's cell phone buzzed on the desk beside his keyboard. His pulse bounced. Let it be Rose. He'd already left two messages for her. He couldn't leave a third. But his hopes were crushed when he recognized Cecil's work phone number on his caller identification. Why was the younger man calling him? Their legal subcommittee had completed their assignment successfully. Donovan was keeping his position as board president. They didn't have anything more to discuss.

"Van Carroll." Donovan wanted to keep this short. He had a lot of work to do. And Rose might be trying to call.

"Van. It's Cecil Lowell."

"What can I do for you, Cecil?" Donovan prodded the conversation along.

"Listen, I got your email this morning with the, uh, city council's response. Nice work."

Other members of the legal subcommittee had responded to the group email. They hadn't felt a need to call Donovan directly; neither had members of the board. Why had Cecil? "Thanks. But this was a team effort. We all did good work."

"Yes, it was a team effort." Cecil's tone seemed to brighten with that concept. "Everyone worked together to make it happen."

"That's right." Donovan straightened as he prepared to end their conversation. "Thanks for calling, Cecil. I've —"

"What would you have done if the board's majority had voted to allow the pawnshop to move in?"

Donovan swallowed a sigh. His gaze drifted toward his office window. It was another beautiful summer day in Columbus. August was coming to an end, taking the worst of the season's heat with it. Fall was only a month away. Rose's law school reunion was even sooner.

His attention returned to Cecil. "If, after reading and discussing the pros and cons of having a pawnshop in the same neighborhood as the shelters, the board had voted in favor of it, I would've accepted the board's decision."

"That's the difference between us. If the

majority of members had disagreed with me, we'd still be debating the issue."

Donovan could believe that. Cecil was stubborn to a fault. "I don't think you would have been president for long."

Cecil snorted. "You're probably right. Just like you're right when you said this was a team effort."

"Yes, everyone worked together to make our case." Donovan checked his watch. He needed to wrap up this call. *Where was Rose?*

"But we couldn't have accomplished this victory for the shelter without your leadership." Cecil's words surprised Donovan.

"Thank you." He couldn't think of anything else to say.

"I realized that the day after the board decided to keep you as president." Cecil chuckled. "You're a good leader. You listen to other opinions instead of trying to get people to do what you think is best."

"I appreciate your saying that." What had gotten into Cecil? He sounded almost mature.

"It's the truth. I'm sorry for not realizing it sooner." Cecil paused. "I'm also sorry for the trouble I've caused the board."

"That's in the past."

"You're a damn decent guy, Van. You're

also a lucky one to have such a talented and successful girlfriend. I wish you both the best."

"Thank you." Donovan didn't feel very lucky. He felt like an idiot — or a lovesick teenager. Why wasn't Rose returning his calls? He didn't know what else to do. If he didn't hear from her by the end of today, he'd show up on her doorstep Saturday morning.

Rose opened the door to find Donovan on her doorstep Saturday morning. She should have known he'd force a confrontation. Donovan Carroll hadn't gotten as far as he had by avoiding conflict.

"I wasn't expecting you." Rose stepped back to let him into her house.

Her eyes skimmed hungrily over his broad shoulders, trim waist and tight glutes. Her body reacted to the memory of those muscles beneath her hands, the feel of his weight pressing against her.

"You haven't returned my calls." Donovan captured her gaze. "What happened?"

Rose caught his scent as she walked past him to lead him to her living room. Her pulse tripped.

"I'm sorry, Van." She made herself face him. "I've decided not to go to my reunion."

228

"What? Why not?" He looked as though that was the last response he'd expected.

"All along, I've had three choices — go alone, attend with a fake boyfriend or not to go at all." Rose spread her arms. "I don't want to go alone. I've never wanted to do that. But I've decided lying is too complicated."

"But you've already lied." Donovan rubbed his forehead. "You've told your friends about me. We had dinner with Maxine and Isiah."

"That was unexpected." *What a tangled web I've woven.*

"What are you going to tell them?"

Rose shrugged. "That we've broken up."

A strange expression moved across Donovan's features. It was gone in a blink. He seemed to stiffen, then relax. "Have you already paid our registration?"

"No, there isn't a deadline for registration." Actually, she'd paid the discounted early registration fee. The law school could consider Donovan's registration a gift to its annual fund.

"What about your panel presentation?"

"There are other people on the panel." Good grief, he had a lot of questions. Rose paced farther across the room.

He gave her a look of such intensity. Rose

was torn between confessing everything and making love to him again. Neither response was appropriate. Instead she waited warily for his next move.

"What does that mean for us?" His voice was low and graveled.

Rose had dreaded that question even as she'd wanted to get it out of the way. She swallowed hard. "I consider that we've fulfilled our business agreement. The city council has responded favorably to the shelter's statement, and I'm no longer going to my reunion."

"Our business agreement? Is that all the past two months have been?" There was no mistaking the anger glowing in his eyes.

"That's what we entered into, yes."

"And what about Thursday night?" Donovan pinned her with his stare. "Was that a clause in the agreement?"

Their one night together had been magical. Donovan Carroll must be the most generous lover on the planet. She'd hold that night in her heart forever and relive it in her fantasies. She would never have a night like that one ever again. Donovan had ruined her for anyone else.

"Thursday night was wonderful. But it can't ever happen again."

She *wasn't* looking for another heartache.

A man who could make a woman feel like that — how long could Rose possibly hope to keep him satisfied?

Rose was ripping out his heart with every syllable that dropped from her luscious lips. Donovan set his jaw and masked his pain with a defiant note. "Why can't we have another night like that one?"

Her eyes widened. She gazed around her stark living room as though searching for an answer. "As wonderful as that night was, I'm not looking for perpetual hookups."

Did she think that's what he was? "What are you looking for?"

Rose spread her arms. "I'm looking for stability, permanence."

"And you don't think I can give you that?" His eyes narrowed as he searched her features.

"A man who makes love like that cannot possibly be monogamous."

Donovan gaped at her. *Is she kidding me?* "Are you critiquing my technique?"

"No, of course not. I'm just saying that you're very sexual, which isn't a bad thing. But I'm not."

Donovan stilled. "There were two people in that bed, Rose. Two very satisfied, very sweaty, very tired people."

Rose planted her hands on her hips and glared at him. "I'm not saying that I regret making love with you. I wanted that night just as much as you did."

"You just don't ever want to be sexually satisfied again. Is that it?" Donovan returned her glare.

"You're ridiculous." Rose threw up her hands and stomped to the other end of the room.

Donovan watched her. Her navy shorts showed off her long runner's legs. Her gray tank top had touches of pink in its pattern. She was adding more color to her outfits. The memory of her lingerie — two scraps of hot-pink cloth — sent the blood rushing to his crotch. What was she wearing today?

Donovan turned and paced to the opposite side of the room. Several deep breaths helped ease his discomfort. He turned, but she still had her back to him. "What's really going on, Rose? Just give me the truth. I want to know."

"The agreement is over."

"Screw the agreement. What about us?"

The pause was long and uncomfortable before she spoke. "There is no 'us,' Van. We're too different."

Donovan stiffened. Those words were painfully similar to claims he'd heard before, most recently from Whitley Maxwell after he'd told her that he and his father had been homeless. Was that the real reason Rose had decided to end all contact with him? She'd told him his past didn't matter to her. Had she lied? Or had someone convinced her that his past should matter?

"I see." Donovan braced his hands on his hips as his body accepted this emotional punch. "I thought you were different, but apparently, I was wrong."

Rose spun to face him. She started to speak, but then seemed to reconsider her words. "I'm sorry, Van. But we might as well end things now before we go any further."

Donovan nodded. "You're right. We should break things off now. I wish you every happiness, Rose."

"You as well, Van."

Donovan marched to her door and let himself out of her house. Happiness had never seemed more elusive. He was three-for-three in the romance department. Every woman with whom he thought he could spend forever had left him once they'd learned about his past. But Rose's rejection hurt the worst. He'd imagined unlimited possibilities with her. With her, he felt he could accomplish anything. Now he wondered what kind of future he could have on his own.

"Donovan and I broke up." Rose made the announcement during her monthly dinner with her former classmates. This would be their last get-together before the reunion, which was only three weeks away.

A chorus of concern circled the booth.

"You two broke up?" Claudia's lips parted in surprise. "When?"

"Last week." Rose kept her responses as close to the truth as possible. Tomorrow would be one week since Donovan had walked out of her house.

"You guys weren't together that long." Tasha arched an eyebrow. "Why'd you break up?"

"Work." She'd anticipated this question. "We both have demanding careers. We weren't able to spend much time together." Hopefully, the story would sound as plausible to her friends as it seemed to her.

"Oh, I'm so sorry to hear that." Maxine shook her head in disappointment. "Isiah and I really liked him."

Me, too. "We're still going to be friends." *If only that were true.*

"Wait a minute." Tasha lowered her glass of iced tea. "Max, you met him? When?"

Maxine shrugged. "Isiah and I ran into

234

Rose and Van at The Cheese Quartet a couple of weeks ago."

"And you didn't tell us?" Tasha's eyes were wide with shock.

Maxine chuckled as she lowered her glass of ice water. "It wasn't like a state supreme court decision or something that would impact our lives or careers. We just had dinner at a pizzeria."

Tasha waved a hand. "Max, you and I need to have a conversation about expectations."

Maxine shared a laughing look with Rose. Tasha's obsession with gossip was well-known. She'd been the same way in law school. It didn't appear that she would ever change.

"Isiah's going to be disappointed that he's not going to know another man at the reunion who he can hang out with while we're busy with reunion activities." Maxine folded her arms on the table.

Their server already had taken away their empty dinner settings. The friends were waiting for their separate bills. But they weren't in a rush. Tonight, the Ethiopian restaurant was especially crowded. Other diners' conversations seemed louder and the scents of exotic spices and well-seasoned meats seemed stronger.

"Your fiancé can spend time with my husband." Tasha tossed the invitation impatiently. "So what are you going to do about the reunion, Rose? Are you still going?"

"Yes, I am." Strangely, she wasn't as bothered by the idea anymore.

Tasha's eyebrows stretched higher. "Alone?"

"It appears so." Rose shrugged.

Tasha looked around the table as though seeking confirmation of what she'd heard. She turned back to Rose. "But what about Ben?"

"What about him?" Rose forced a smile, hoping to soften the challenge in her tone. She didn't need Tasha to remind her that the problem of Benjamin still existed. However, now, Benjamin and his pregnant wife didn't feel like a problem. When had that change occurred and what had caused it?

A lightbulb came on in her brain. Not *what* had caused it; *who* — Donovan. He'd made her feel important and desirable after Benjamin's treatment had made her feel less than.

"Rose isn't the only one who's going to the reunion alone." Claudia interrupted the exchange.

Tasha turned to Claudia. "Claud, I realize

236

there's going to be other single alumni there."

"Including me." Claudia took a drink of her iced tea. "I signed the divorce papers last week. Rose and I will both be flying solo."

"Oh, Claudia, I'm so sorry." Rose's heart went out to the other woman.

"Me, too." Maxine reached across the table and squeezed Claudia's hand.

"Thank you." Claudia inclined her head.

"Hold on, Claud." Tasha raised her right hand, palm out. "You *signed* the papers last week? When did you *file* the papers?"

"Earlier in the summer." Claudia shifted on her seat.

"And you're only now telling us?" Tasha swept a hand to include Maxine and Rose.

Claudia met Tasha's gaze. "Sometimes, I don't want to gossip about my life. There are things that happen to me that I want to process on my own without other people giving me their opinions. Sometimes people give things more importance than is necessary."

Rose blinked. "That's what happened to me. I was so concerned about what other people would think about Ben and me seeing each other again at the reunion that I almost decided against going."

"What changed your mind?" Maxine asked.

"Van did, of course." Tasha snorted. "He's fine. He makes Ben look like yesterday's news."

"That's how I felt at first." Rose remembered Lily's words. "But then I realized that my reaction was giving Ben and other people too much power. It doesn't matter what anyone else thinks. I don't need a man to validate me."

Why hadn't I recognized sooner the truth in what Lily had said?

"Well, that's convenient, especially since now you *are* going to the reunion alone." Tasha studied her black polished nails.

Claudia gave Rose a searching look. "You're sure you and Van have broken up? There's no chance of your getting back together with him?"

"I'm sure." It hurt to say the words. Adjusting to life without Donovan was a million times more painful than getting over Benjamin, even though she'd been with her ex-fiancé much longer.

Claudia leaned into the table. "Would you have a problem with my giving Donovan a call once my divorce is final?"

Rose blinked at Claudia. "Yes, I would." Had the other woman lost her mind?

"Well, then why are you letting him go?" Claudia's shrug was philosophical. "If you want him, hold on to him."

Holding on to him wasn't a healthy idea. Rose wanted Donovan, but she couldn't see the charming player as her happily-ever-after.

Donovan looked up at the knock on his office door on Monday afternoon, the last day of August. He stood when he recognized Iris in the threshold. She was a vision in her gold dress. "You look like a bright summer day."

"And you look like you need some cheering up." Iris paused on the other side of his guest chairs. "What's wrong?"

Donovan liked Iris a lot, but today it was hard to look at her. The resemblance between her and Rose was so strong. There were subtle differences in the sisters' appearances — Rose's features were more elegant while Iris was more exotic. But both women were tall and slender with shoulder-length dark brown hair. Iris's hair was wavy while Rose's style was bone straight. It would probably be a very long time before Donovan could look at Iris without thinking about Rose.

"Nothing's wrong." Donovan motioned

toward his computer monitor. "I'm just trying to work out some sales proposals."

Iris followed his gesture. "You don't usually look depressed over your sales proposals."

"It's a particularly challenging one." Donovan smiled reluctantly at Iris's persistence. Despite her nod of understanding, he had the sense she wasn't buying his cover story.

"I'm on my way to meet Ty for lunch, but I wanted to drop off the proposal for the sales campaign and rollout schedule." She passed him the manila folder she'd carried into his office. "Let me know what adjustments you want me to make or if you need clarification on anything."

Donovan took the folder from her. "I'm sure it's perfect, like your other proposals."

"Thank you, Van. I hope it is." Iris hesitated. "It seems that Xavier's gotten over his breakup with his girlfriend. I asked Ty whether that was true. But I thought I'd ask you as well since you're usually more observant."

"Ty's better at noticing the world around him now, thanks to you. He actually steps away from his desk and talks to people face-to-face occasionally."

"It's nice to hear that I've had a positive impact on him." Iris's cheeks grew pink.

240

"Ty thinks Xavier has recovered. What do you think?"

"Are you concerned because of Xavier's obvious interest in Lily?"

"You've noticed that, as well?" Iris sat on one of the guest chairs in front of Donovan's desk.

"I don't think Xavier's trying to be subtle." Donovan dropped onto his executive seat.

"Let's hope not because, if he is, he's failing miserably." Iris chuckled. "In fact, I think the only person who hasn't noticed is Lily."

Donovan grinned. "Are you going to tell her?"

"Rose doesn't think we should. I think she wants to be there when Lily finally realizes it on her own."

At the mention of Rose, Donovan's chest tightened. His grin faded and he sat straighter on his chair. "You don't have anything to worry about. Xavier wouldn't ask Lily out if he was still hung up on his ex-girlfriend. We're not players."

Iris gave him a curious look. "I know that. You men are the good guys."

"Thank you." *How can I convince Rose of that?*

"Are you and Rose ready for her reunion?"

241

Iris got to her feet. "It's less than three weeks away."

Donovan stood with her. "Rose isn't going to her reunion." Iris's question caught Donovan off guard. Surely, Rose had told her sisters that she'd changed her mind about the event. The three women were so close.

"Yes, she is. She made me sit through a run-through of her panel presentation the other night." Iris made a face. "What makes you think she isn't?"

"Because that's what she told me." Donovan crossed his arms over his chest. *What was going on?*

Iris blinked her surprise. "You must have misunderstood."

"I'm sure that I didn't."

"Why would she tell you that she isn't going if she is?"

"I'll ask her."

CHAPTER 13

"Van, is something wrong?" Rose let Donovan into her house on Monday evening.

She hadn't expected to see him again so soon. With Iris dating one of Donovan's best friends and Xavier making eyes at Lily, she knew she couldn't avoid Donovan forever. But she'd hoped to have a bit more time to prepare herself. Right now, her pulse was beating so fast she couldn't catch her breath.

Donovan turned to face her. "You lied to me."

She crossed into the living room. Donovan followed her. Her mind was racing for a response. There wasn't any point in lying again. He'd only call her on it. Besides she didn't like lying to him at all.

"Who told you?" She sat on the sofa, gesturing for Donovan to take the love seat.

"Does it matter?" Donovan folded his long, lean frame onto the black leather love seat.

"No, it doesn't. I was just curious."

"So am I." Leaning forward, Donovan balanced his elbows on his thighs. "Why did you lie about attending your reunion?"

She didn't want to lie to Donovan, but she didn't want to tell him that she was afraid of falling in love with him, either. "I didn't want you to feel obligated to attend the reunion with me. That's why I told you that you'd fulfilled our business agreement."

"Why wouldn't you want me to attend the reunion with you?"

Because I didn't want to see you flirt with my former classmates.

Rose looked into his troubled hazel eyes. She scanned the clean lines of his classically handsome sienna features. He made her heart jump. "I'm going to attend it alone. The lies were becoming too complicated."

"But we've invested so much time and energy into developing our fake relationship."

"Yes, and I'm sorry about that." Though not completely. She regretted the heartache that was giving her sleepless nights, but she couldn't regret the time she'd spent getting to know him.

"Then why are you leaving me behind? What have I done wrong?"

"You haven't done *anything* wrong." Rose

rushed to reassure Donovan. "This isn't about you." Not exactly.

"Then what is it about?"

Rose stood and crossed to her fireplace. "It's about me." Her mind raced ahead for the explanation. "I didn't want to hide behind one man to make another man jealous. That would be childish."

"But it didn't seem childish before?"

"No, it didn't." Rose rubbed her left shoulder, trying to ease the tension. "I guess the time we spent together helped me realize that."

Donovan frowned. "You think I helped you see that?"

"Yes, I do."

"Then why don't you want to make our fake relationship real?"

She'd opened the door to that question, the only question she didn't want him to ask her ever again. "We're too different, Van." Dear God, she wished they weren't.

"How are we different?" Donovan stood, shoving his fists into the front pockets of his navy cargo shorts. "Is it my past? You told me it didn't matter to you that I'd been homeless for a year and a half as a kid, but it does matter, doesn't it?"

"No." Rose wouldn't allow him to think that of her or of himself. "How could you possibly think that of me? I told you that I was impressed by you and all you've accomplished. I lied about attending my reunion. That was wrong and I'm sorry. But I didn't lie when I said I don't think less of you because of your past."

"If this doesn't have anything to do with my past, then I don't see how we're that different."

"Van, I wish you'd just accept my decision to end our relationship — all versions of it." Rose wrapped her arms around her waist. "I don't think it would work out between us. And that's my decision."

The silence was heavy between them. The tension built. Finally, Donovan nodded once. "All right, I'll accept your decision. Goodbye, Rose."

Rose swallowed the thick lump in her throat. "Goodbye, Van. And thank you for everything."

"Of course." His gaze lingered on her face a moment longer.

Rose watched as he turned to leave again; this time, for good. As her front door closed behind him, she let her tears flow.

"Earth to Van. Are you with us, pal?" Tyler's teasing broke through Donovan's consciousness.

"Sorry. What did I miss?"

It was early the next morning, the first day of September. Donovan sat with Tyler and Xavier in Xavier's office. But his mind kept replaying his conversation with Rose from the night before.

"Sleep." Xavier sipped his coffee from the huge company mug.

"Xavier's right." Tyler's forehead was creased with concern. "You look terrible. And this toxic substance you call coffee doesn't seem to be helping."

"It might if he drank it." Xavier gestured toward Donovan's mug.

Donovan glanced at the mug of coffee balanced on his lap. It was practically full. Yet he knew the brew was strong. Its scent permeated Xavier's office.

His friends were right. He hadn't been able to settle down last night. Rose, her reunion and their lovemaking had circled his mind like a gam of sharks.

"What's on your mind?" Xavier asked.

Rose wasn't the first woman to break up with him. But the end of their relationship was the hardest to face. *Was that because she meant the most to me?*

"Rose broke up with me." Donovan left his mug on a corner of Xavier's desk and stood to wander the almost painfully neat office. "It sounds ridiculous, doesn't it? How do you 'break up' a fake relationship?"

"It started out fake, but it was obvious that you developed feelings for her." Tyler's voice carried from behind Donovan.

"I didn't think I would. My first impression of her wasn't great. Then I realized she was tough on the outside, but kind, caring, brilliant and funny on the inside. Now I can't get her out of my mind." Donovan rubbed his eyes with the heels of his hands, trying to banish the images of Rose that bedeviled him.

"What happened between you?" Xavier's question wasn't that easy to answer.

"I don't know." Donovan had spent a sleepless night, wondering the same thing.

"Did you ask her?" Xavier sounded as baffled as Donovan felt.

Donovan stopped in front of Xavier's office window. Thin strips of clouds drifted across an azure sky. The image was a backdrop for more visions of Rose: her chocolate eyes, beautiful smile and brilliant presence that lit up a room despite the dark, oppressive colors of her wardrobe. When he closed his eyes he could smell her scent, feel her skin as soft as silk against his palm.

"She told me she wasn't going to her reunion. I later found out that was a lie."

Donovan scowled at the view from the fifth-floor window. "When I confronted her, she said a fake relationship was too complicated to keep track of."

"She has a point." Xavier's voice was thoughtful.

"I agree," Tyler said.

"So do I." Donovan turned away from the window and walked past his chair and Xavier's glass-and-metal conversation table. "But my not going to the reunion doesn't mean we have to stop seeing each other."

"Then why did she break things off?" Tyler shifted on his gray cushioned seat to face Donovan.

"All she'd say is that she believes we're too different." The more Donovan mulled over Rose's reasoning, the more irritated he became. It wasn't true that they were "too different." They had a lot in common.

"How are you different?" Xavier asked.

Donovan rubbed his forehead. "She wouldn't give examples."

"Then that's not the real reason." Tyler's response was the realization Donovan had come to overnight. Rose was lying. But why?

"Do you want to know why she broke up with you?" Xavier's dark eyes pinned Donovan as though trying to read his mind.

"Yes. I know I'm not the only one who

developed real feelings in this make-believe relationship."

"Then ask her again." Xavier leaned back on his black leather executive chair, balancing his coffee mug on his right knee.

Donovan shook his head. "I've already asked her more than once and in different ways. She won't come clean with me."

"She must have told her sisters how she feels. Do you want me to ask Iris?" Tyler's offer was tempting.

"No, thanks." Donovan rubbed his forehead. "I don't want to put anyone in the middle."

"What do you want to do?" Xavier studied Donovan as they waited for his response.

He didn't have an answer. "I think the reason she ended things is that she's afraid to trust me."

"Why?" Tyler's voice held a defensive note as though he was the one being attacked.

"She doesn't want to get hurt again." Donovan blew a frustrated breath. "Rose broke up with her ex-fiancé when she found out he was cheating on her. She thinks I'll do the same thing."

Xavier arched an eyebrow. "Do you really want a relationship with someone who doesn't trust you? You'll have to prove yourself every day."

Tyler sighed. "That would get really old really fast, Van."

"I want a relationship with Rose." Donovan looked from Tyler to Xavier. "That means I need to convince her to trust me."

Xavier spread his hands. "How?"

"I don't know yet." But he had to try. He'd rather spend his future proving himself to her than spend his future without her.

"Why did you tell Van you weren't going to your reunion?" Iris got straight to the point when Rose answered her cell phone on Tuesday evening.

Lightbulbs came on in Rose's mind. "*You're* the one who told Van I was still going."

"Maybe if you'd let me in on your plan, I wouldn't have given away your secret." Iris's response was wrapped in irritation.

"If I'd told you what I was going to do, you would've talked me out of it." Rose imagined her sister curled up on her chunky emerald sofa — or perhaps her matching love seat — as Iris chided her.

Rose was certain she was right. Iris was faithful to family, but she also was loyal to friends. She would have tried to convince Rose not to mislead Donovan. But Rose believed what she had done was right for

251

everyone in the long run.

"Why did you tell him you weren't going?" Iris returned to the question at hand. She'd always been stubborn, even as a child.

"Things were getting complicated. I thought it would be easier for Van and me if we scrapped the whole reunion idea."

"But you're going alone."

"That's right." Rose sat up on her black leather sofa and laid the romantic suspense novel she'd been reading on her coffee table. She hadn't been able to concentrate on it, anyway. Thoughts of Donovan kept intruding: his voice, his smile, his scent, the weight of his body on hers.

"I thought you didn't want to go alone. That was the whole point of my introducing you to Van in the first place." Iris's words brought Rose back to their discussion. "What happened? Did Ben and his wife get divorced?"

"Not that I know of."

"Then what?"

Rose stood and crossed to her living room's front windows. "I didn't want to get involved with another player."

"A player?" Iris's voice rose in disbelief. "Van? How many times do I have to tell you he's *not* a player?"

Rose planted her right hand on her hip

and tightened her grip on her cell phone. "You may know Van as a friend, but I know him as a boyfriend. Well, a pretend one."

"His character is the same. Van has loyalty and integrity. That doesn't change when his libido switches on."

Through the sheer curtains of her front windows, Rose stared at the quiet neighborhood outside her home in Columbus's Short North area. The evening shadows were growing longer. She could see one of the entrances to Goodale Park.

Rose massaged the tense muscles at the nape of her neck. "Women ogle him wherever he goes."

"He's handsome, successful and charming. There's a lot to admire."

"The afternoon you and I had lunch with Ty and Van, every woman in the diner was staring at him — and at Ty."

"I don't blame them." Iris's tone was dry.

Rose frowned. "That doesn't bother you?"

"Were either Ty or Van staring back?"

"No."

"Then it shouldn't bother you, either."

Memories of the times she and Donovan had gone out together in public streamed across her mind: coffee at the café when they'd agreed to work together, the impromptu lunch when he'd bought her roses, the celebratory dinner with Maxine and Isiah at the pizzeria. Each time, Donovan had received second and third looks from more than one woman, but he hadn't appeared to notice the attention. Instead, his focus had been on Rose. His gaze, his smiles, his touches had been only for her. Still . . .

"You're right. The attention he gets from other women shouldn't bother me, but it does." Rose turned away from the window and crossed back to her sofa.

"Van really likes you, Rosie," Iris softened her tone. "I can tell by the way he talks about you. I could see it when we had those family dinners. He's a great guy. Give him a chance."

Rose's determination wavered under Iris's words. Her head and her heart were on opposite sides of this debate. She had to remind herself of the risks. "Claudia's getting a divorce."

"I'm sorry to hear that." Iris seemed confused by the apparent change in subject.

"When I told her Van and I broke up, she asked if she could call him. I don't want to have to worry about the women waiting in the wings for my relationship to fall apart."

"Then don't." Iris sighed. "Rosie, I know Ben hurt you. But you can't condemn all men because of one jerk's actions."

"What do you want me to do, Iris?"

"I want you to stop standing in the way of your own happiness." Iris's words were sharp with impatience. Right about now, her baby sister had probably uncurled from her sofa and was pacing her own living room in her town house nearby.

"I'm not standing in my way." Rose dropped onto her sofa. "I'm protecting myself."

"To what end, Rose? Do you even know?"

"What do you mean?" She was losing patience with Iris's arguments. "You're spending a lot of time and energy defending Van. Why don't you use some of that energy to try to understand how *I'm* feeling, little sister?"

"I'm not defending Van. I'm trying to help you."

"How?"

"Why won't you listen?"

"Because every word out of your mouth is a criticism."

"Rose, *you're* the one who said Ben had ruined the plans you'd had for yourself — marriage and children." Iris's urgency forced itself down the phone line. "You have another shot at those things with Van."

"Van? Why would I even *consider* that

with a man who's a carbon copy of Ben?"

"But. He's. Not. Will you *listen*?"

Rose's heart wanted to, but her head was shouting them both down. "Iris, I can't have this conversation with you." She sighed, pushing herself to her feet again. "You and I have very different perspectives on romance. I'm glad you've never experienced what I have, and I hope you never do. I'm protecting myself the best way that I know how to."

"You've taken it too far. I don't want you to end up alone just because you're too stubborn to know a good thing when he walks into your life."

"I don't need a man to make me happy. I'm not afraid to be alone." Better to be alone than to experience another broken heart. And this time it would be a thousand times worse if Donovan was the one to break it.

"You're running scared, Rosie. That's not like you." Iris's accusation stung.

"It's not fear. It's wisdom from experience."

"Whatever. I hope you come to your senses before you lose a good thing."

On whose side was her sister? "Goodbye, Iris. Thanks for the call."

"Get some sleep, Rosie."

Rose ended the call, then returned to her sofa. Iris was wrong; she wasn't running scared. She was being cautious. Yes, she missed Donovan. She missed him so much it was killing her. But calling off the relationship now was smarter than waiting for him to end it.

Wasn't it?

"You were right, Lil." Rose sat on the other side of the table from Lily at the downtown restaurant where they were having lunch on Wednesday afternoon.

"That's always nice to hear." Lily drove her fork into her garden salad. "What was I right about this time?"

Rose looked around the popular lunch spot. It was located midway between their jobs. It was fortunate they'd arrived early. The crowd of customers waiting to be seated extended to the doorway.

She turned back to her barely touched burger and fries. "I was giving Ben too much power. I was letting my reaction to him and his new wife, and his soon-to-be family dictate how I would spend my reunion. That was stupid."

"Yes, it was." Lily took a sip of her ice water with lemon. "But don't be so hard on yourself. It's understandable."

"I have a hard time believing you'd make the same mistake." Rose dipped a steak fry in a pool of ketchup.

"Ha. Don't bet on that. It's always easier to see the solution to *someone else's* problem."

"You should tell that to Iris." Rose still stung from last night's argument with her youngest sister. "She thinks I'm handling this entire situation with Van wrong."

"Why? What are you doing?"

"I've decided not to go to my reunion with him." She sipped her iced tea. "I'm going to go alone."

"Why?"

Rose looked up in surprise. "I thought you'd be happy with that decision. It's what you recommended from the beginning."

"It doesn't matter what *I* think." Lily forked up more salad. "It's your reunion."

Rose stared at Lily. She admired her sister's Zen-like behavior, but sometimes it made her a little crazy. "I decided I didn't have to bring a guy to my reunion as a measure of my worth or success. Like you said, I'm successful on my own."

"I'm glad you've realized that."

"Iris thinks I broke things off with Van because I'm running scared."

"From what?"

258

"From having my heart broken. And she's right. But am I wrong for not wanting to go through that again?"

"Of course not."

"I'm glad someone understands." Rose dragged the fry through her ketchup. "I have to protect myself."

"I do understand. But I think you're both wrong." Lily finished her salad.

Rose blinked. She hadn't expected Lily's comment. Their server arrived to refill Lily's glass of ice water and top off Rose's iced tea. She waited until the young woman left with Lily's empty salad bowl before continuing their conversation. "What are we wrong about?"

Lily met her gaze. "Rosie, you're right. Ben is a pig."

"I know." Where was Lily going with this?

"For him to sleep with all of those women, even while you were planning your wedding, was reprehensible. He didn't only damage your trust in men. He damaged your trust in yourself. The reason you continue to lump all men in the same category as Ben is that you're afraid to trust your instincts."

Rose gasped. The truth of what Lily was saying was a sucker punch to her gut. *Why hadn't I realized it before?*

She braced her elbows on the table and

held her head in her hands. Rose felt sick. "For Pete's sake, Lil. Do you really think so?"

"Of course I do."

"That son of a —"

"The good news is your self-confidence is coming back." Lily pulled her bowl of chicken noodle soup closer. Rose caught a whiff of its seasonings.

"Can I get you ladies anything else?" Their server appeared with the bill folder.

"Nothing for me." Lily gestured toward Rose's untouched burger. "But we'll take a to-go box."

Rose returned her attention to Lily as their server disappeared again. "What makes you think I'm getting my confidence back?"

Lily seemed surprised by Rose's question. "You're going to the reunion by yourself."

"You think that's a good thing?"

"I think it's a step in the right direction." Lily dug into her purse for her wallet.

Rose took the bill folder. "I'll put this on my card."

"This is for my part of the bill and tip." Lily gave Rose her money.

Rose put Lily's money in her wallet and tucked her credit card into the bill folder. The server appeared on cue. She left the to-go box and took the bill.

"Iris thinks I should go with Van to the reunion." Rose transferred her burger and what was left of her fries from her plate to the to-go box.

"One step at a time." Lily's tone became chiding. "But if you and Iris spent less time *telling* each other what to do and more time *listening* to each other, you'd find your conversations much more pleasant."

"You're probably right." Rose drained her glass of iced tea.

The server returned with Rose's card and receipt. She thanked them for coming before vanishing again.

"Of course I'm right." Lily collected her purse. "You're both bullies, and you both always think you're right."

"We don't bully *you*." Rose followed her sister from the restaurant.

"That's because I don't let you."

The restaurant was in walking distance of both of their downtown offices. On the sidewalk, Rose prepared to part ways with her sister. "What did you mean by 'one step at a time'?"

"The first step was finding the confidence to go to the reunion by yourself." Lily adjusted her purse strap on her shoulder. "The second step is allowing yourself to fall in love with Van."

"What?" Shock rocked Rose back on her heels.

Lily gave Rose's forearm a quick squeeze. "He's a good person and seems to genuinely care about you."

Rose shook her head. The thought of taking that risk was overwhelming. "I don't know, Lil."

Her sister smiled. "Trust your instincts, Rosie. This time, listen to your heart and tell your head to shut up."

She watched Lily disappear into downtown's lunch crowd. Rose was still reeling from Lily's insights but her sister was right. She'd blamed herself for making the mistake of trusting Benjamin. That error in judgment was the reason she no longer trusted her instincts. And it was the reason she was afraid to love Donovan.

Now that she recognized what was holding her back, could she find the courage to fall in love?

CHAPTER 14

The knocking broke Donovan's concentration on Wednesday afternoon. Kayla stood in his office doorway. She'd accessorized her pink business dress with a pearl necklace and matching earrings. Her hand was raised as though she was preparing to knock again.

Donovan stood. "Kayla, hi. Please come in."

"Where were you?" Kayla's onyx eyes twinkled at him. She settled onto his guest chair.

"What do you mean?" Donovan circled his desk to sit beside her.

"I knocked twice before." Kayla cast her gaze around his office. Unlike everyone else, she didn't have a noticeable reaction to the papers strewn across most of his office furnishings. She was probably used to the sight by now. Her attention lingered on the photo of him, Xavier and Tyler posing in their caps and gowns after their college graduation.

"I'm sorry. I was lost in thought." Embarrassment warmed Donovan's cheeks.

"I could tell." Kayla's soft laughter was warm with affection. She drew her gaze from the graduation photo and settled it on him. "What were you thinking about?"

"Work." His flush deepened.

"Work, huh?" The look in Kayla's eyes told him she didn't buy it. Fortunately, she changed the subject. "I'm here to personally invite you to my annual Farewell to Summer Barbecue. Can you attend?"

Donovan relaxed. "I wouldn't miss it for the world. Thank you."

It was startling to realize they were already halfway through September. The formal invitations to Kayla's fete had been mailed in August. Still, every year, Kayla visited each department at Anderson Adventures to invite associates and their families to the Farewell to Summer Barbecue held at her house. Her personal attention ensured that most people attended, which meant she hosted more than two hundred guests. Afterward, the company always experienced a boost in morale — and productivity — which carried them into the holidays and the next big Anderson Adventures social event. Donovan didn't think Kayla held the barbecue for business reasons, though. She just enjoyed a good party.

"Wonderful." She reached over to pat his hand. "You're welcome to bring Rose, of course. How is she?"

Donovan drew a steadying breath. He inhaled her scent, a soft fruity fragrance. Foster had bought her the perfume. "We're no longer together."

The twinkle faded from Kayla's eyes. "Van, I'm so sorry. What happened?"

"Things didn't work out." He lowered his gaze to her hand on his.

"What things?" She squeezed his hand.

Again, he wished he had the answer to that. "I don't know. She wouldn't tell me."

Kayla seemed to take that in. Her silence as she held his hand was both comforting and supportive. Donovan disappeared into his thoughts until she spoke.

"I didn't like Xavier's last girlfriend." Kayla's comment came out of nowhere, but Donovan went with it.

"That was obvious to everyone but Xavier. And Ty." He grinned.

Kayla's slender shoulders shook with her chuckles. "Before Iris, Ty couldn't see anything outside of his computer monitor. Although, to his credit, he never missed a family birthday or holiday."

"No, he didn't."

"I didn't like Lauren because she was secretive." Kayla shook her head in disapproval. "You can't trust secretive people."

"Lauren proved that."

"On the other hand, Rose and her sisters are open books. You know where you stand with them, and you know what they're thinking — because they tell you." Kayla tilted her head. "Lily's the quiet one, though. She lets her sisters do most of the talking."

"I've always admired your powers of observation." Donovan turned his hand to hold hers.

"But you have no idea why I'm telling you this, do you?" Her dark eyes twinkled at him again.

"No, I don't." Donovan struggled against a grin.

"We agreed that Rose is an open book. So she must have a pretty big reason not to tell you why she called things off."

"Like what?" Donovan searched Kayla's eyes. He was desperate for an answer. Did she know? If so, he wished she'd just tell him.

"Think about it, Van. Why would someone not tell you something?"

"I don't know. Because they're afraid?"

"Bingo." She winked at him.

"But she doesn't have any reason to be afraid." He heard the frustration in his own voice. "How do I convince her to trust me?"

"You could start by trusting *her.*" Kayla released his hand. She crossed her legs and smoothed the hem of her dress over her knee.

"I do trust her." Donovan's eyes widened in surprise.

Kayla arched a perfectly shaped eyebrow. "Then why haven't you told her how you feel?"

"I told her I wanted to continue our relationship." Wasn't that the same thing?

"Oh, Van." Kayla shook her head in disappointment. "Why do couples always play the game of Who Will Say I Love You First? It wastes so much time."

"You think I should tell her?" Donovan's throat was dry. Rose already had rejected him twice. He didn't think he could survive hearing no from her a third time.

"If she's The One, go after her and tell her how you feel." She leaned forward to cup the side of his face. "If you don't, the alternative is to spend the rest of your life with regret."

The thought of spending the rest of his life without Rose filled him with fear. The feeling was even stronger than the panic he felt at the idea of telling Rose how he felt.

Donovan drew another deep breath. "Thank you for the advice, Kayla. You're right. I don't want to live my life with regret. I'll talk with Rose."

"Wonderful." Kayla patted his hand. "If the Anderson Adventures men play their cards right, I'll have the pleasure of helping to plan several weddings next year."

"Including your own?" Donovan stood with her.

Kayla winked as she returned his smile. "If he plays his cards right."

The company's matriarch waved as she left his office. Donovan returned to his desk. If he was going to avoid living a life filled with regret, the first thing he needed to do was make plans to spend the weekend in Ann Arbor, Michigan. He had a reunion to attend.

"Hi, Lil. I'm at the hotel." Rose spoke into her cell phone. She lifted her weekend travel bag onto the suitcase stand at the foot of the king-size bed. The room was spacious and well maintained — and freezing.

"Great. Thanks for letting me know." Lily's response carried down the line. "How was the drive?"

268

"Long and uneventful. And long." Rose went to the thermostat beside the window and turned down the air-conditioning. It had been set at sixty degrees, not a comfortable climate for her navy capris and lavender tank.

"I'm glad you made it safely. Have you checked in?"

"Yes, I'm all set. I'm in the hotel room now. I'm going to unpack, then see if anyone I know has arrived. I'll call Iris first, though, to let her know that I got here safely."

"I hope you have a good time. What's your room number?"

Rose's eyebrows knitted in curiosity. "It's 238. But if you need to reach me, just call me on my cell phone. You don't have to go through the front desk."

"Okay." Lily seemed distracted. What was she doing?

"I'd better get going. I want to register tonight."

"Wait a minute. I can call Iris to let her know you arrived safely, if you'd like. You have a lot to do."

"That would be great. Give her my best, and tell her I'll call her in the morning."

Lily kept Rose on the phone a while longer asking what seemed like unnecessary questions. Rose grew anxious to end their call.

Then a knock on the door startled Rose. "Lil, there's someone at the door. I'll check in with you tomorrow. I'd better go now. Take care."

Once she'd ended the call with her sister, Rose went to the door, leaning in to look through the security peephole. She gasped when she recognized the person on the other side of her door. Her pulse kicked up. She couldn't catch her breath.

Rose freed the locks, then pulled open her door. She blinked, but Donovan didn't disappear. "You're not supposed to be here."

"Is that any way to greet a friend?" He arched an eyebrow at her. On him, the expression was too sexy for words.

Rose was frozen to the spot. She still couldn't catch her breath. Why was this happening now? She wanted to see him, to talk with him, but she needed more time to prepare.

"What are you doing here?" Her gaze ate him up. In his casual dark slacks and jewel-toned polo shirt, he looked like an ad for a wicked weekend.

His hazel eyes moved over her face as though he hadn't seen her in years rather than weeks. "We need to talk, Rose. May I come in?"

"Van, that wouldn't be a good idea." Rose swallowed hard, remembering the king-size bed that dominated the room behind her. "How did you know which room I was in?"

"I had a little help from Lily."

Rose's confusion cleared. Now she understood why Lily had asked her room number and kept her on the phone for so long. A good sister would have warned her. "Both of my sisters seem very fond of you."

"I like them, too."

"Good. Tell them I said hello when you get back to Columbus." Rose started to close the door. She needed more time.

Donovan pushed against it to keep it open. "Rose, please. Just give me five minutes of your time." He made a show of looking up and down the hallway. "You don't want to cause a scene for your classmates, do you?"

Donovan had a point. She didn't want her classmates to see her and her ex–pretend boyfriend engaged in a shoving match with her hotel door. The idea of inviting him into a room with a king-size bed didn't sit well with her, but it was the lesser of two evils. Her time was up. Rose stood back to let him in.

"Thank you." Donovan strode past her,

tempting her with his scent.

Rose locked the door, then turned to face him. The room didn't seem as spacious anymore.

"Please say what you have to say, then leave." Rose crossed her arms, trying to keep her anxiety from spreading. "Although I don't know what you have to say that's so important that you had to drive to Ann Arbor rather than pick up the phone."

"I'm in love with you."

The air rushed out of Rose's lungs. The blood drained from her head. She locked her knees to keep from collapsing onto the floor. "What?"

Donovan closed the distance between them. He held her upper arms and stared down into her face. "I drove three hours so that I could tell you in person that I'm in love with you, Rose Beharie."

Rose stepped back from his embrace. She needed room to think. Her legs shook as she walked past him, then dropped onto the bed. She studied the thin gray carpet as she struggled to gather her thoughts. "You can't be in love with me. We were pretending to be in love."

"I know the difference between real and make-believe, Rose. When you told me you didn't want to see me anymore, the pain I felt was very real."

Rose looked up at him. She remembered her own pain when she made that decision. "But we've only known each other three months."

Donovan took a step toward her. "And how long do we need to be together before we admit what we already know?"

She'd lived with Benjamin for two years before she'd realized their relationship wasn't about love. It was about something far less romantic: Benjamin and his needs. After three months, she was more in love Donovan than she'd ever been with Benjamin.

"I want to believe that this will last." Her eyes sought his.

Donovan went down on his knees in front of her and took her hands in his large, strong ones. "Give us a chance, Rose. That's all I'm asking. Would it really be so horrible to fall in love with me?"

The look in his hazel eyes mesmerized her. He already had her heart. With the slightest nudge, he could have her body and soul. All she had to do was trust her instincts.

But how can I? Her head was still spinning. "Suppose you get bored with me?"

Donovan chuckled. "You could never bore me. You turn my world upside down. You fascinate and confound me. You arouse me and occasionally irritate me. But you will never bore me."

Rose gave him a skeptical look. "I won't compete with other women."

"I'm not asking you to." Donovan raised her left hand to his heart. "You're the only woman for me, Rose. It's you or no one. Sweetheart, I need you to trust me."

More than his words, the look in his eyes said it all. He wanted to spend forever with her, and she wanted the same thing. Tears stung her eyes. Her heart was full to bursting.

Rose freed her right hand to cup the side of his handsome face. "I've already fallen in love with you, Van."

His eyes widened with surprise. "You have?"

Rose smiled. "When I met you, I wanted revenge against my ex-fiancé. But falling in love with you has been so much better than revenge."

Donovan pulled her off the bed and into his arms. He pressed his lips to hers. Her body flooded with warmth and desire. Falling in love was indeed so much sweeter than revenge. And all she had to do was trust her instincts to find her happily-ever-after with her very own hero.

ABOUT THE AUTHOR

Regina Hart is the contemporary romance pseudonym of award-winning author Patricia Sargeant. Her various pastimes and hobbies include sports — both college and pros — movies, music and, of course, reading. She loves chatting with readers. Contact her at BooksbyPatricia@yahoo.com. You can also friend her on Facebook as Patricia Sargeant/Regina Hart.

The employees of Thorndike Press hope you have enjoyed this Large Print book. All our Thorndike, Wheeler, and Kennebec Large Print titles are designed for easy reading, and all our books are made to last. Other Thorndike Press Large Print books are available at your library, through selected bookstores, or directly from us.

For information about titles, please call:
  (800) 223-1244

or visit our Web site at:
  http://gale.cengage.com/thorndike

To share your comments, please write:
Publisher
Thorndike Press
10 Water St., Suite 310
Waterville, ME 04901